I0727926

HE HEARS THE SILENCE

GENE GALLIEN

Copyright © *Gene Gallien,* 2025

All Rights Reserved

This book is subject to the condition that no part of this book is to be reproduced, transmitted in any form or means; electronic or mechanical, stored in a retrieval system, photocopied, recorded, scanned, or otherwise. Any of these actions require the proper written permission of the author.

Vieux Carre'

Lloyd and Lester: Lloyd was born and raised in New Orleans and knew
Every street and dark alley. While working offshore he was in an accident
And his back was broken. After a very large insurance settlement he decided
To become a private investigator. He hooks up with Lester, a homeless
Veteran and what they can't solve together can't be done.

Table of Contents

Chapter 1
One The Streets

As the fog is rolling off the Mississippi River into the French Quarter and the morning sun is trying to break thru, he hears footsteps behind him as he is walking down Royal Street to Esplanade Ave. He continues walking at a slow pace, and then in a split second, he moves to this right and his follower hits the street face first with a knife in one hand and some sort of club in the other. Lloyd puts his foot on the guy's throat, takes his knife and breaks the blade off and lays the pieces on the guy's face and says, "You should not be trying that because you just might get hurt very bad."

Now that the sun is starting to break thru the misty fog, he decides to ease over behind the French Market and walk along the banks of the river and then head to his apartment that is behind Pete's Restaurant and bar and can be accessed from two different streets. It's small and quaint, and it is all he wants or needs.

He is still really upset about his niece being robbed and killed the night she was celebrating having just graduated from Newman College and as she was going to her celebration, someone somehow managed to strangle, rob and kill her.

There were hardly any witnesses, and nothing was on any of the security cameras on the local businesses.

Everyone knew Lloyd. He is friends with the district attorney, the Mayor, police chief. Lt. Governor, state attorney general and all the city policemen, as well as the FBI. He had barely stayed on the good side of the law and he was a registered private investigator and was always armed.

As he is starting to head to his apartment, he stops and tries to stretch his injured back. He had hurt his back in an oilfield accident one summer while working offshore, trying to make money for law school.

Now that it is carnival time, he usually goes to Biloxi for a couple of weeks and then comes back home after all the partying is over. Last year, while he was there, he had won a little over ten thousand dollars, and he had it hidden in his apartment, and he was high tech because he could see his apartment from both streets where the cameras were hidden.

When he was in Biloxi, he would walk the beaches at night. While there, his phone could pick up all the movements around his apartment.

He sees Pee Wee putting something on his front door and says to himself, "it can wait until after the carnival is over."

Now that carnival is over and everyone has left town, he rides the bus back with three hundred dollars less than what he went over there with. Not too bad for being there for two weeks. He had given them their money back.

He gets to his apartment, and the note is from Pee Wee saying that the streets are talking and that someone has pawned a necklace with a diamond in it at a pawn shop in Slidell.

The next day, he and Pee Wee rent a car and go across the lake and find the local pawn store. He sees the necklace in the showcase and asks the kid behind the counter if he could see it.

When he takes it, he says, "OK son, I want to know who pawned this and when."

The kid behind the counter says that he cannot give him that information without his boss being there, and he is out of town. In a split-second, Lloyd has the kid by the collar of his shirt and halfway across the counter and before Lloyd could say anything, the kid was saying I will get you that information if you will just put me down.

When they get the info, they drive to a rather run-down looking area. Cars and trucks up on blocks, trailers with tarps covering half of their roofs, and a slew of other things. They sit and wait and right at five o'clock, a not so clean, rather heavy-set guy drives up on a motorcycle and goes in a trailer.

Their plans were to return tomorrow in a different car and work their plan. Sure enough, right at five, a big boy shows up, and Pee Wee walks up to him and asks him if he is the guy who has a motorcycle for sale.

Before he could say anything, Lloyd deployed his favorite working tool, a garrot. Once he tightens it, the big boy goes to the ground, and they cuff him. They had a really hard time getting him in the back seat of the rental car, but finally managed.

As they are driving back across the causeway, he calls the district attorney at home and tells him that he has the number one suspect in the death of his niece and that he will be dropping him off at the central lockup and to please call and tell them that I am on my way.

When they got to the central lockup, there were about six policemen standing by the drop-off place for prisoners. When he drives up, they all clap and say, way to go, Lloyd and Pee Wee. The guy's help get big boy into lockup, and he had to go in and fill out a bunch of forms and get his cuffs back.

Before he does anything else, he gets in contact with all the bail bondsmen in the city and tells them not to let anyone bond him out because he is pretty sure this is the guy that killed his niece.

Not wanting his name and picture all over the TV stations and picture in the paper, he lets Pee Wee get the credit for finding and capturing big boy.

The whole city is abuzz because of how and when she was killed, and Crime Stoppers had offered a ten-thousand-dollar reward for just the capture. He gets the money and keeps it because he had spent more than that paying for her funeral.

Once again, he becomes the Night Walker as he was called most of the time because the streets talk more at night than in the daytime. He walks in all the different neighborhoods. The rich in uptown to the ones not so rich downtown in the nineth ward. Most all the homeless people are afraid of him, and when they see him walking towards them, they usually pick up their stuff and take off. He loves it.

When he walks in the dense fog, he is usually whistling a very low and eerie sound.

Being a nondrinker, when he goes in a bar in the French quarter, they always serve a soft drink in a dark glass and no one can tell what he is drinking and if there happens to be a lady of the night in the bar, when he goes in, they leave.

In his trade, as he refers to it, he tries not to break any laws but at times he must come close and manages to stay one step ahead of everyone.

Early one morning just as the sun is breaking over the river, he is sitting on a bench in Jackson Square with no one around. He sees a guy walking toward him, and he keeps looking around like he is afraid someone is following him.

As he gets closer, Lloyd puts his phone on record and waits and watches and the guy sits down beside him and asks, "Are you junior?" and he says, "Yes I am." The guy hands him a package and says, "This is the package that the president of the dock workers union has ordered, and when you deliver it to him, he will give you the twenty five thousand dollars because we could only get thirty six fake passports and not the forty that he wanted but we can get more later."

The guy leaves and calls his buddy at the FBI and says, "Coffee Broadway Street." He gets up and starts walking to the corner of Canal and Broad Street to the Coffee House.

When he gets there, he gets in the agent's car and tells him the complete story from start to finish. He has done enough work with them that he knows the system. The agent leaves and he goes in and has a nice breakfast and just sits and listens to what everyone is saying.

The big conversation is about the ball game Sunday between the Eagles and their beloved Indians. One more win and they are eligible for the Super Bowl playoffs.

Since he had been up all night, he thought he would ease back to his apartment and get a little rest because one never knows what the streets will be doing or talking about.

He always carries two phones with him because if an agent needed to talk to him, he could always answer that phone and sure enough the red phone rings and the guy says, "Well, good morning lover boy, what's going on?"

He tells him that he was asleep and whatever he wants better be good. They agree to meet in the cemetery at the end of Canal Street at four o'clock and they will visit their favorite grave to talk.

After he has showered and gotten dressed, he thinks to himself, "I think I will start carrying my new Glock forty-three pistol." He slips it in the holster behind his back and walks to Canal Street and catches a streetcar. He is at the graveyard in ten minutes and heads out to kneel and pray at the grave, where he meets a lot of the federal agents.

He has no idea who he is praying for, but maybe he will be looking over him. He thinks and then laughs to himself.

As he looks up, he sees someone that he has never seen before and gets nervous and moves his gun to his side so that he can get to it more easily if he needs to use it.

Mr. unknown says, "Lloyd, it's ok, it's me, Tommy." He breathes a little easier and asks him what in the world is he doing in disguise? He tells him that they have been watching a guy who they think he may be involved with the passport thing that you just happen to be at the right place at the right time.

The person that we are looking for has his house for sale, and I am going with a real estate lady to look at his house and just in case he happens to be there, he won't recognize me because these guys have pictures of every agent in town.

As they are talking, the agent tells him that there is a new group of bad guys that have just formed across the river, and we want you to try and join up with them and to keep us posted on what their plans are and to get their license plate numbers.

The more he listens to the agent, he figures out that it is a national organization that doesn't like a certain race of people and can be some bad dudes. As they are leaving, the agent gives him a paper, and he just puts it in his pocket and waits for another streetcar.

While he is waiting, he reads the paper, and it is an application to join the boys across the river with a post office box number. He is thinking now do I really want to get involved in this, or just stay away but the pay is good and in cash.

On the way home, he stops and gets himself something to eat and sees some of his normal Quarter people and they can just sit and talk for hours about everything and nothing at all except for the next ball game. Half of them have no idea what they are even trying to say about it. They all know that he is a night person, and they are asking why is he out while it is still daylight?

He goes to his apartment and looks at the application and decides to fill it out using a dead guy's name and his post office box number. He does not want any of his mail delivered to this apartment because there are too many thieves living around him.

As he is filling it out, he decides to use the phone that the agents use just to be safe, and when it rings, it can only be one of two people. He drops it in the mailbox around the corner and just happens to see an old friend who had been sent to prison a few years ago for attempted murder of a guy who was dating his wife.

When he sees him, he says, "Hey Spike, what are you doing out of the can?" and says, "I thought you got twenty years?"

Spike tells him that he got out in seven because of good behavior and that he oversaw his unit's bible study. Lloyd goes crazy laughing and says, 'What, and are you telling me the truth?" He tells him that yes, he is telling the truth, and he will not be trying to save his lazy ass.

Lloyd says, "Man it was saved a long time ago because I was laying in that hospital bed, not knowing if I would ever be able to walk again after I hurt my back, and I asked for help and I got it, so I am a true believer. Getting hurt scared the devil out of me, so I am ok at this time, and I think I need a refresher course. I will call you."

Spike tells him that he has gotten a job on the docks as a runner doing just about everything that they need taken care of between the three different offices and I can fill in as a laborer when they are shorthanded. He thinks, "My, my, what good news that is."

It's midnight and he is having coffee and Beignets at the French market when one of his U S Marshall friends comes and sits with him. They talk about football and what the home team will do if they make the playoffs and if any of them had heard anything about the missing little girl from the projects. He had spent a lot of time asking questions and trying to follow up on any leads about the little girl.

The Marshall slides him a piece of paper with the name Rick Bell on it. As they keep talking, Lloyd writes on it. Relatives in Westminster, MD.

They finish their coffee and go their separate ways.

He decides to take a walk along the riverbank and then down the levee, where all the old empty warehouses are, just to see if he can run into any of his regular nighttime friends and pick up on any gossip.

Sure enough he runs across Dolly, a forty-year-old female who looks like she is eighty, and she is smoking a joint and offers him a hit. He refuses and asks her, "What has been going on?" She says, "You got some Georges with you." (Georges are one-dollar bills) He tells her that he has a couple and asks her what she has got.

After a couple of minutes, she says, "You know that big, tall Indian looking feller that has been hanging around the Fifth Street projects?" he tells her yes, he remembers seeing him sitting on the bench by Rusty's place, why, he asks? She then says to him, "Do you remember when the little girl went missing from the projects? Ding Dong told me that he grabbed her, and she has not been seen since. He gets a cold chill and really doesn't know what to do."

He asks her how she knows that, she stops and looks at him, and then says, "You know the streets talk, now get out of here and go bother someone else and give me my Georges." He gives her a ten-dollar bill and moves into the darkness.

As he is walking onto St. Charles, he is thinking, how does she know that, and if it is true and if he is hanging around the projects again, something better be done. His mind is racing, and he is totally confused and wants to go and find the guy and drop him where he is sitting.

Now that it is just about daybreak, he decides to give the chief of police a call and have him meet him at Lee circle. He gives him a call and when he answers, Lloyd says, "Lee Circle in thirty and hangs up."

In twenty-five minutes, the chief pulls up and he gets in the car with him. He hasn't even taken time to put his uniform on. As the chief is driving around the central business district. Lloyd says, "Broad and Iberville." They don't talk much on the way.

As they pass that spot, Lloyd looks all around and then he says, "Pull over." The chief nearly hit the curb while pulling over so fast.

The chief says, "You are killing me, what do you have? and it better be good, or you are in big trouble?"

He says, "You know the little girl that came up missing from the projects, and the chief says "Yes, and it is killing me and if you have anything worthwhile, you will be king of Mardi Gras."

Lloyd says, "You know that big, tall guy that is around Canal and Broad, he's your guy, and that comes from the streets and where I got it from is only about one hundred percent right." He gets out of the car and vanishes into the quarter and goes home to bed.

He decides to come out around nine and check the streets out. With the game in town, the streets will start getting busy about now when all the out-of-town people hit the Quarter. Since there will be so many drunks around, he decides to go back to bed and come out later.

When he hears the street sweepers, he knows that the crowds are gone, and he decides to see what is going on, but he is going to go back and see Dolly later and then he goes into Smithy's All-Night place and gets a couple of Bologna turnovers and a root beer. He stays at Smitty's for a while, discussing football, local people, the missing little girl and then he is out the door headed to the river levee.

As he gets close to where Dolly hangs out, he can hear her screaming and yelling and saying, "Leave me alone, I don't have any money, and quit hitting me."

He eases into the area where this guy is roughing up Dolly, and he takes his pistol and hits the guy just below his ear, and he is down. Not moving but breathing. Then he picks him up and gives him a straight kick in the gut and then throws him out of the warehouse onto some old railroad tracks.

He shows Dolly a hand full of ten-dollar bills and says, "You want, you got to talk to me now, or I'm going to finish what that guy started." After looking at him for a minute, she usually tells him what he asks for.

She tells him that the big guy had given Donny some girls' clothes to get rid of for him, and after that he ended up in the river and he had told me that. Then she said that he had told her that the big guy had figured out how to get under the Coliseum floor, and that is where he lives and even has fixed some wires so that he has electricity, and I think he is the one who put Donny in the river.

He tells her, "Ok, here is a hundred, and do you want it all now or a little at a time?" She tells him to give her twenty and not to forget where she is.

Living under the Coliseum and has electricity, guess we better check this little bit of info out and if he is the one that took that little girl, I want to be the one that takes care of him he says to himself as he is headed to St. Charles Avenue.

Once again, he calls the chief of police and says the same thing, "Lee Circle thirty, and hangs up."

When he gets in the chief's car, all he says is, "Where is your notepad, and let's go eat." As they are riding, he is writing and then they go into the coffee shop, he tells the chief to order him something and he keeps writing. When they bring his food, he closes the tablet and says, hi chief, how are we doing? He says, Lloyd, you are killing me and what in the hell have you written?

He says, "Do you want to try and read it in here or a little later when we are in the car?" He says the car will do, and they start talking football and continue eating.

They go and get in his car, and the chief turns the overhead light on and starts reading. The more he reads, the more he grunts and groans and starts cussing under his breath and when he lays the pad down, he looks at Lloyd and says, "Thanks buddy, and we will have him before the next full moon." Then he adds, "Whatever that is."

The chief drops him off in the quarter and once again, he is gone.

He had gone to bed after the chief dropped him off and had just gotten up and sees that it was two o'clock and it's too early to hit the streets, so he decides to read for a while. He tries to read his bible a couple of hours every day. As he is reading, his phone rings and he sees that it is one of his street buddies, Skeeter.

When he answers, Skeeter is talking so fast that he can't understand him and he finally understands what he is saying, he is telling him to turn the TV on because they think they have found the person that possibly kidnapped the little girl from the projects and the guy was living under the Coliseum and when they searched the place, they found one of her flip flops.

After he hangs up, he says, "Way to go Dolly."

The city is buzzing with good news, and everyone keeps asking the chief how they were able to crack the case, he says that he cannot give out that information, but adds, "Have you ever heard the saying, 'The streets talk'?Our streets spoke loud and clear on this, and whoever it was that figured out that this might be our guy needs to be king of carnival."

After three weeks of legal paperwork and witnesses, the trial started for the guy accused of killing the little girl. By the time his trial was over, he had been convicted of kidnapping and first-degree murder. He was sentenced to death and the judge asked the state to try and carry out his sentence as soon as possible.

He decides to go out and when he does, he finds the streets flooded with football fans from Atlanta and he just stands around casually just watching the people having a good time. As he is walking around, he remembers that he had filled out some type of form to join up with the bad guys across the river and he better go to the post office and check his mail.

Yep, there it is, he has been approved to join up with the Brotherhood of Tomorrow. He calls Tommy, the agent that got him involved in this and tells him that he is now an active member of the Brotherhood of Tomorrow, and they are having a meeting across the river Thursday night at seven o'clock.

He goes to his storage building and gets his motorcycle out and fires it up. He rarely rides it but starts it up regularly. As he is letting it run, he is saying to himself, "I wonder where this neighborhood is, and I wonder if my bike will be safe, and I will park it so that if I must leave in a hurry. I will be able to bail out."

Thursday comes around and he is ready to join the club and heads across the river. He has googled the address, and it is in a very dark area close to the ferry landing. He has his nine-millimeter pistol in a holster in the small of his back.

When he arrives, the leader he guesses is Todd Mayes and he introduces him to all the guys that are already there. He counts seven others so if he must resort to using his gun, he will have just enough rounds to put everyone down.

The city is buzzing with good news, and everyone keeps asking the chief how they were able to crack the case, he says that he cannot give out that information, but adds, "Have you ever heard the saying, 'The streets talk'?Our streets spoke loud and clear on this, and whoever it was that figured out that this might be our guy needs to be king of carnival."

When Todd tells everyone to stand and salute the club flag, he thinks to himself, Oh, me, what do we have here? The meeting lasts an hour, and he asks Todd if there are any dues or anything. Todd explains, "After you've been a member for three months, you must pay one hundred dollars into the party kitty."

As soon as he puts his bike up, he calls Tommy and asks him if there or any other of his or agents going to the same meetings as he is, and he swears that he is the only one, just in case he must hurt someone he did not want to be a good guy.

The temperature is dropping, so he decides to go and get some coffee and just hang out, and then take it in for the night. While standing by the Royal Hotel, he sees his old girlfriend, Mattie. She tells him that the vice squad has really been hitting the quarter hard to try and catch us asking patrons to buy us a drink and these football hookers are something else. She tells him that these out-of-town girls are really hurting the local workers.

He then asks her how her little boy is doing, who is at St. Jude Hospital in Memphis. She tells him that he is responding to treatments and the doctors are saying that it's great news. He tells her that he sends money there every month, and she tells him that if she could afford to go, she would go up there and give her ex-mother-in-law a break.

He asks, "When do you want to go?" Then adds, "I've got a friend who owes me a favor. He'd be glad to drive you. And here's five hundred."

She says, "Tomorrow would be great."

She starts crying and hugging him and saying, "Really? You're not messing with me, are you?" He says, "When it's that serious, I don't joke." Then he adds, "I'll go talk to your boss. You'll still have your job when you get back. And since you don't have to pay for food or lodging, this five hundred is just in case you need some walking-around money. Be right here at nine o'clock in the morning."

He calls the chief of police and explains that Mattie's situations she needs a ride to Memphis because her little boy is in St. Jude. The chief asks, "Where do we pick her up?" He gives him the location and replies, "Thanks, Chief."

Not being able to sleep much during the day, he decides to get up and go across the river and visit his ex-in-laws, the parents of the niece who was robbed and killed, since he has not seen them since her funeral and just to see how they are doing.

After a good visit, he decides to head back across the river, but before he does, he needs to get gas and stops at the closest gas station to fill up and get a snack. When he goes inside, he sees one of the guys who was in the meeting the other night and they strike up a conversation while no one else is in the area.

By the time he is ready to leave, he finds that Steve was kicked out of the Army, had served seven years for armed robbery, and is on probation for eight more years and has several guns in his trailer.

Being a felon, Lloyd knows that this guy is not supposed to have any guns anywhere around him and thinks that he just might be carrying as he is talking with him. He makes up his mind that if something starts to go bad at one of the meetings, this guy is the first one to get capped.

This Sunday, with the game out of town, the quarter is quiet, and he is still up from the night and he decides to go and listen to the guy that calls himself The Quarter Savior, and he preaches in the sitting area by the coffee house. As he walks up, he is surprised to see about thirty people listening to him and singing along with his three-piece band that is with him.

Being raised in the church, he knows quite a bit about the bible and decides just to sit and listen for a while and see who is there also. He knows most everyone by having seen them around town and there is a couple that he does not know, and he makes a mental note about a guy's red hair.

As the church breaks up, he sees Spike and they start talking about his new job working or the dock board and how he liked it. He tells him that he likes it because he is always busy doing something, going from office to office and then down on the dock delivering packages and meeting different people off the ships.

He says something that gets his attention when he says, "You know, there are a lot of tourists that get off some of the freighters, and most of them are from Iraq and places like that."

Lloyd asks, "Do you ever see them get back on the same ships?" Spike shakes his head. "Nope. Can't say I have." They go and have some breakfast, and Spike is talking all the time about everything and nothing of much importance, except the tourist thing.

He gives Tommy, his agent friend, a call and tells him what he has learned from Spike and that just might have been where the false passports were headed.

Later in the week, just as the sun is starting to break through the fog and he is sitting in Jackson Square, he sees this rather large guy in a suit walking towards him and he thinks, I don't have my gun and what is this guy doing at daybreak in a suit in the quarter.

The man walks up and asks, "Do you sit here a lot?" Lloyd replies cautiously, "Yeah, I do. Why?"

The man lowers his voice and asks,

"Did a guy ever walk up and give you a package… then just walk away?"

Without missing a beat, Lloyd replies, , Yeah, a pretty good time ago when I was sitting here and that a real tall guy arrested for kidnapping and sent to Angola to be fried for killing the little girl was sitting on that bench over there and I saw a guy give him some kind of package and walk away and I was wondering what they had going."

The man narrows his eyes. "Are you sure?" Lloyd says, "If I tell you a rooster can pull a freight train, just go to the depot and watch." The big guy walks off, wondering what he has just heard.

Since Spike owes him a favor for saving his life a few years ago, anytime something is different or something he can't get a handle on, he always comes to Lloyd for an answer. Sure enough, something odd is taking place, and he goes looking for him.

He finds Lloyd and says, One of the guys in the office under the bridge has asked me to go to the docks in Baton Rouge and meet a small ship from Columbia delivering bananas and pick up some frozen banana seeds and bring them back." Lloyd raises an eyebrow. "Frozen banana seeds? What in the world would anyone want with frozen banana seeds?" Spike shrugs. "That's what I said."

Lloyd replies, "Maybe he's planning to grow banana trees."

Later, Lloyd calls his agent friend, Tommy, and tells him what Spike just shared. Tommy instructs him, "Ride up there with him. I'll have one of our agents meet you, and they'll bring a portable X-ray machine. We'll scan the package before it's delivered."

On the way back to New Orleans, they get stopped for speeding. One of the state troopers steps up and asks, "Mind if we search the car?" Spike and Lloyd's hearts stop, and Lloyd says calmly, "Sir, before you do, I need to make a phone call. I'm not giving you permission to search."

He calls Tommy and says, "State troopers have stopped us. Here, talk to him." He hands the phone to the trooper, and in less than a minute the trooper hands him his phone back and says, "Have a nice day, guys. Be safe," and waves them on.

Once they deliver the package, Lloyd turns to Spike. "Keep up the good work. I'll see you later."

During his thinking time as he calls it, these dock people have a lot going on and it's just not placing ships for unloading or taking on freight, they are bringing in people with false passports and doing a little drug work with the banana growers and he hopes Spike can keep up the good work and not get caught helping him and the big boys.

Usually, the weather is decent in New Orleans but there is a cold front coming in and the Quarter will be vacant for a few days so he decides to catch the bus to Biloxi and try his hand at the crap table and if he isn't doing that, he is somewhere where he can hear what's going on and he keeps a keen eye out for New Orleans people that just might be over there.

While checking out the casino, he finds a pool room and it is full of people laughing and playing pool and snooker. Being an avid player, he manages to get into conversations with a bunch of different people, especially an African American guy who shoots a mean stick at the tables.

The young guy introduces himself as Daniel Cook, and he has just gotten out of the army and is taking some time off just going around the country before he gets serious about finding a job. They continue playing until the early morning hours and plan to hook up again sometime later today.

For some reason, Lloyd does not buy his story, especially when he notices a bulge in the small of his back. He says to himself, "DEA, and there must be something going on the coast if he is here." He calls Tommy and asks, "Check if there's a DEA agent named Daniel Cook— young, African American, slight New England accent."

They meet up again for lunch and just have a general discussion, mostly about sports. He really knows a lot about most sports. Then they get into personal stuff like where are you from, what college, where you served, and just general conversation.

As they are playing Snooker and Daniel is leaning over the table getting ready to make a shot, Lloyd gets right by his ear and whispers, "You need to do something about that hump just above your belt on your back." Before he could say or think, Lloyd says, "You shoot a mean stick for being a DEA."

Then Lloyd says, "I might have been born in the dark, but it wasn't last night," and he says, "it's still your shot."

Daniel breaks up laughing and must put his pool stick down and says, "Let's go get a beer." As they are sitting in a back corner booth, Lloyd says, "Daniel Cook. Cincinnati, Ohio. Ohio State University. Ran track. Degree in general studies. Preparing for law school. Never served a day in the Army."

Daniel freezes for a second, then smiles and says, "You know something? When I first met you in the pool parlor, I thought, This guy looks like a smart-ass."

They both laugh.

Daniel continues, "The Truth is, I was nervous around you. I couldn't figure you out. And you shoot a mean game of pool."

Lloyd leans back. "That's probably all you'll ever know about me. Now give me your number—because someday, I'm gonna put you on something that'll make you a hero."

Daniel writes down his number. Lloyd pockets it, stands up, and walks away.

After a few days of doing nothing but gambling, he decides to go back to the Big Easy and see what has been going on because there is always something happening, good or bad.

On the bus, he is pretending to be sleeping. He hears these two guys talking about meeting a guy by the name of Shorty. He knows Shorty, and whatever these guys are planning on doing, it won't be good because anyone doing business with him is up to no good.

After listening to these guys talk, he figures out that they are from Mobile, and they have something to do with stealing cars and putting them on ships, and shipping them overseas. Another insurance scam dreamed up by Shorty.

When the bus starts unloading, he still pretends to be sleeping and he sneaks a look at where the guys go and sure enough, they get in one of Shorty's many cars and they drive away.

The weather has warmed up quite a bit and the city was waking up and as always and the streets are buzzing with locals and tourists when a local plain clothes city detective drives up and says for him to get in his car. As they ride around and head out for lunch, the detective asks him all sorts of questions trying to find out what is going on in the city.

As usual, he gives him just enough information to keep him guessing what is real and what is just air. When something goes down in the city, the first person that the local and federal agents find him and asks him if he knew what happened. Most of the time, he manages to dance around their questions and leave them guessing.

After getting his mail, he finally gets home and decides to take a much-needed nap and come back out when it gets dark.

When he gets up, he sees that he has a text from Mattie and one from Todd, the bad guy across the river. He calls Mattie first, and she tells him that she just wanted to let him know that her little boy is doing much better since she has been with him, and she really appreciates what she has done for him and that she is planning on staying up there for a couple of months.

Then he answers Todd's text by saying, "What's up? Todd replies by saying that they were going to have a meeting, but they had to call it off because one of the club members got arrested for some kind of drug dealing.

"Drug deal," he says to himself. He calls Spike and suggests that they have breakfast tomorrow, and he agrees. After a visit with Dolly and the sun starting to break through the morning mist, he heads out to meet Spike at Canal and Broad.

Spike says that the only thing he heard was that the guy from the mail room came in and said that to ship those banana seeds to New York by special delivery was going to cost forty dollars, and was he sure that he wanted to do that. The office manager yells at the poor guy and tells him to mind his own business and do as he is told.

He decides to jerk Daniel's chain and sends him a text saying, "Banana tree seeds." Later, before he puts his phone down, he gets a text back saying, "What in the world is this about banana tree seeds?" He answers him back by saying, "Later."

He tells Spike to find out what kind of car the office manager drives and to get his plate number and send it to him. Spike just smiles and says, "Oh boy, I wonder what is going to happen next."

The local news is going crazy about the guy who had kidnapped the little girl from the projects had admitted to the crime and by admitting to the crime, and now is asking the state's attorney general not give him the death penalty but one hundred years in Angola. The attorney general said no way and we are trying to move up your death date.

With everything that was happening, he decides to go and visit Dolly and give her a few Washingtons to help her get by. When he finds her, he cannot wake her up? She is still breathing, and her body is cold and sweaty. He calls nine one one and tells them where she is and leaves the old warehouse.

The next morning, he checks with his sources at the hospital, and he finds out that she has had a stroke, and they don't know if she will make it or not. He says a prayer for her well-being and whatever the final thing is, he can live with it, and he knows that she has a relative somewhere in Mississippi but has no idea who or where.

When he gets up, he goes to the hospital and asks, "What they did with her clothes?" and they told him that they are in a plastic bag under her bed in the ICU. Then he tells them that he is her uncle and wants to go through what she was wearing, and someone said, "I hope you can stand the smell."

He tells them to go and bring him the bag and not to worry about the smell because she is a human being, and that she had better be getting good care.

As he is going through her tattered clothes, he finds a little piece of paper rolled up real tight. When he unrolls it, he sees a number written down. It is an area code for Mississippi, and he decides to call it.

When a man answers, Lloyd says, "Hi, this is Lloyd in New Orleans. I am a friend of Dolly, and who am I speaking to? The guy says, "Charlie and I am Dolly's brother, and now what's she got herself into? Lloyd tells him, "She is not in any trouble, but she has had a major stroke and may not make it."

Her brother says, "She had donated her body to Tulane Med school a few years ago. On that same piece of paper, there should be three letters showing DNR.

Before Lloyd could say anything, the brother adds, "Thanks for calling," and hung up.

Not knowing what to do, he goes back to the hospital and gets in touch with a doctor who is on call and explains what the brother has said, and before anything else is said, he tells Lloyd that she had died about two hours ago. After he gets over the shock, he manages to tell the doctor that she had donated her body to Tulane Medical School and walks away.

As he is walking back to his apartment, he is saying to himself, "Maybe I should donate my body because I really don't have any family, and they might be able to cure some dreaded disease by using it. I will check into that later."

While checking his mail, he gets a call from Spike telling him that he must deliver a package to a guy at the Casino in Biloxi, and did he wanted to ride over there with him. He asks, "When and what Casino, and where in the casino were they to meet?"

Spike replies, "It's at the Big Dice Casino. I'm supposed to meet a chick at the pizza restaurant at five o'clock. That's four and a half hours from now, we can take our time once we hit the road."

As soon as he gets off the phone with Spike, he calls Daniel, the DEA guy he had met earlier in Biloxi. When Daniel answers, he asks him where he is. Daniel says, "I'm south of McComb, headed to Biloxi." Lloyd fills him in. "There's a meeting at five o'clock at the pizza restaurant in the Big Dice Casino. Spike's supposed to meet some chick—Dixie, I think—and that's all I know right now."

Then he tells him what Spike looks like and what he will be wearing, and that he will be sitting at another table away from Spike.

Daniel tells him that he will meet up with them after their meeting, but if he decides to follow the chick, just wait for him in the pool parlor.

They get to Biloxi with plenty of time to spare and Spike loses all his money playing craps, and Lloyd had to give him a few dollars so he wouldn't be completely broke and could not pay for his Pizza.

Spike is ordering himself a pizza when the chick walks up and says, "I hope you aren't ordering one with onions." He says, "No, just cheese and veggies." She says, "Great and hi, my name is Dixie, and you must be Spike?" He says, "Yep, you have hit a home run."

As they are talking, Daniel is walking by and spills his pizza and drink all over their table, and all hell breaks loose. Dixie is jumping up, and Spike does not know what to do, and Lloyd is in the corner laughing. Daniel is apologizing and helping Dixie get coke and cheese off her clothes, and Spike is trying to salvage some of his pizza on the table.

Finally, all three of them are talking and have ordered another pizza. Daniel is playing it real cool, and he keeps telling Dixie that he wants to pay for her dress being cleaned and offers to buy her dinner in the Casino any night that she would like.

She thanks him and tells him, "I'm engaged, and my boyfriend might not like it if I went to dinner with a single guy, I am guessing." Daniel replies, "You are right, and I am sorry about your dress, and I must meet a guy in the pool parlor and have a nice day."

About an hour later, Spike comes into the pool parlor, and when he sees Lloyd and Daniel talking, he did not know what to think. They found out that Dixie works for the state director of transportation, and when she got the package, she asked Spike if these were banana seeds. He told her that he had no idea what was in the package.

So, now, someone who works for the state department of transportation is in the business of moving drugs. This could turn out to be something big, and Lloyd does not want to have any part of it, and Spike and Daniel are on their own.

When they get back to the City, he calls Tommy his agent friend and brings him up to date on what happened and that he had put a DEA agent onto it and he was washing his hands of the deal and then Tommy tells him good because there are some rumblings about one of your club members really whipped a member of Gonzales club and they are really a bunch of radicals.

He says to himself, "Why do I let these other people always get me in these tight spots, but the money is good, and I just might need a little excitement in my life."

With it getting close to March seventeenth and all the Irish will be drinking and partying, the pickpockets will be working the quarter strong since they did not have a good run at this year's Mardi Gras. Each year, he works with the police department trying to catch the bad guys.

He walks around with a big wallet chained to his belt and when someone puts their hand on it, his earpiece buzzes and he automatically spins around and puts the bad person on the ground and cuffs them and calls the station in the quarter and he tells them that there is a person laying on the sidewalk and he gives them the address and moves into the crowd.

The partying goes on for usually four or five days, and once the bad guys know they are being watched and their family members are still in jail, the pick pocket business really slows down and then some local decides that he just might try that little scam and before he knew it, he is in jail with the real crooks.

His red phone rings, and he sees that it is Todd, the main guy from the club across the river tells him that they will be having another meeting Sunday night at the same place, and they will be discussing some important business. Just a word of caution, there is no telling what just might happen.

Once again, he thinks, "Now what have I gotten myself into, and I damn sure don't want to get shot or hurt being in an undercover situation." He says to himself, "I am calling Tommy and telling him that I will help him at any time he needs it, but this has just gotten out of hand, and after this meeting, I am out."

When he gets across the river at the meeting place, he decides to park his bike a block away in the walkway of a church where no one can see it. As he goes into the meeting, there are some guys there that he has never seen before, but he sees Steve, the local guy working at the C store.

He manages to sit by a window that has a fan just stuck into it, and it's running, and more people are coming in. He counts thirteen guys, including himself and Todd. The fan is not doing much good.

When he opens the meeting, everyone stands and chants some unknown words that no one can understand. Then everyone sits and is side by side because of the number of guys there.

Todd is standing and telling them that since one of our members whipped the president of the Gonzales club, they have said that there will be blood shed because of what happened and then he says, "We are going to have to go to Gonzales in the dark of night and really do some harm to that club to show them who is boss in this part of the state."

While Todd is running off at the mouth, Lloyd hears what sounds like a truck pull up and turn the motor off, and he hears four doors shut. Not slammed but pushed shut.

He checks and sees that the window fan is just sitting there with nothing holding it in the best he could tell, and he slips his pistol out from behind his back and puts it under his leg with his hand on it.

Suddenly, someone bust the door down and throw a smoke grenade in the room and started shooting, automatically he feels a hot burning pain in his left shoulder and then he takes dead aim that the two guys in the doorway and fires two shots and then he pushed the fan out the window and crawls out and heads to his motorcycle.

He knows that he has been shot, and when he gets his bike started, he heads to the Westside hospital as he is going to the hospital. Police cars are headed in the direction of the meeting.

When he gets to the ER, he tells the nurse that he has been shot once for sure and does not know if he was hit anywhere else. As she is getting onto him a bed, he calls Tommy and says, "Westside hospital now."

The first thing the ER nurse does is call the local police and tell them that they have a gunshot victim, and then she asks him, "What kind of insurance did he have?" He told her he did not have any. She said, "Oh my goodness, we have another one who won't probably pay."

Two local policemen come in and start right away, hitting him with one question after another. He tells them that the pain shot the nurse gave him has made him sleepy and he really can't think too clearly at this time, and they just keep on asking him questions.

The ER doctor comes in and tells them to get out and to wait outside. The doctor tells him that he wants an X-ray to be sure that there was no bone damaged when the bullet passed through under his left armpit.

Just as they are going to take the X-ray, Tommy walks in and shows his badge, and he says, "I will take over from here," and says, "Let's go buddy. Before the doctor or X-ray tech could say anything, they were out the door."

Tommy had brought another agent with him, and Lloyd gave him the bike keys, and they all headed across the river back to the city and when they arrived at City Hospital, there was a group just waiting for them.

As he was checked out by the doctors, he was told that the bullet missed all the bones around his shoulder and that he was very lucky, and he shouldn't be playing with guns. He failed to see the humor in their statements.

He goes to his apartment and goes to bed.

The next day, all the local news stations are reporting on the shooting across the river and that four people were dead and three others injured that they knew of, and possibly one had taken himself to a local hospital.

After a few days' rest, he decides to take a walk around the city to see what was going on and if there was any new gossip on the streets at night.

Sure enough, he sees Lester, an African American who has been homeless most all his adult life and when he has news, most of the time he is right on.

They decide to go and have coffee at the French Market and catch up on what's going on in the city. As they are talking, he sees the guy who gave him the package with the passports in it and asks Lester who he is.

He tells him that his name is Gary, and he works for his uncle, who is the big boss man over everything that goes on around the docks and always carries a gun. Gun was the last thing he wanted to hear.

Lester goes on to say that he had heard that he was having something to do with getting people from other countries into the United States and that they are making millions of dollars each month and at one time had something to do with bringing in drugs from South America.

As he is talking, he wonders what Lester's background is. He has known him for years and has never asked him, and now seems to be a good time.

He does and Lester tells him, "I was born and raised in Memphis by my mother because my daddy left one day and never came back. My mother was a nurse, and when she was at work, I stayed with my grandmother."

In high school, he was a star football player and had numerous college offers and decided to stay in Memphis and go to school there so he could be close to his family.

Lloyd asks him what his major was in school, and he tells him that he was majoring in Pharmacy and had a three-point-five GPA, and in his junior year he was running with the wrong crowd and got into some real big-time trouble. To stay out of the state pen, he made a deal with the judge and if he would go into the military, he would not send him away for a long time and so, that is what I did and got hurt several times and was discharged.

Then I did not know how to do anything after and my grandmother and mother had passed and somehow, I ended up here in the city and on the streets.

He asks him did he know the big guy that killed the little girl, and did he have any idea what he did with her body. Lester says, "Man, I wish you had not asked me that question."

Finally, he gets a faraway look in his eyes and as he is looking at the river he says, "I knew all along that he had kidnapped her, and I figured that the police would not believe me because of my past and memory problems." Then he says, "I am sure that he put her in the river because he was down there all the time fishing and just throwing rocks and one day, I saw him carrying a big rock with him going to the spot where he always sat when he was fishing."

Then he says, "Please don't ask me anything else about that, ok?" "Got it," Lloyd says, and then they go off on something else.

All along, he is getting more interested in what is going on between the people working at the docks having anything to do with the people in Mississippi but whatever it is, he is not going to get so involved that he might get shot again. One time was enough for that.

The next day, Tommy calls him and tells him to meet him at the Oyster bar at five o'clock and they will talk about what happened across the river because of the people getting killed.

When they meet, Tommy tells him that they had a guy in the Gonzales group and had missed a couple of meetings and that they had no idea that they were coming to town preparing to have a gun battle with the local group.

Both guys from Gonzales were shot in the head and the other two guys from your club were shot with a shotgun and the two wounded were hit with pistol fire. Both Gonzales guys were the shotgun shooters and were carrying stolen guns and the third shooter was firing from behind them and when they both went down, he was the shooter who wounded the two locals.

Then Lloyd says, "You can count me out of going to any more meetings when it comes to these nuts. I am willing to help all I can, but no more bad guy things." Then he tells him about the drug thing between the dock people and the Mississippi transportation offices, and Tommy says, "Yes, I know because there is a DEA agent right in the middle of it."

Lloyd says, "Yep, I know, his name is Daniel, and he is an African American and the nephew of a big guy at the dock board, and his name is Gary."

Tommy says, "I should have known that he would know something about the whole scheme of things." He asks him where PEE WEE was because he might ask him to do some work for us at the airport.

He tells him that the last time he talked to him, he said that he was going to Little Rock to stay with his grandmother because he had been messing around with one of the bar maids at Busters and her boyfriend was after him but if you really need to talk to him, I will have him call you.

After they finish their talk and meal, he goes back to his apartment and calls Mattie to see how her little boy is doing in Memphis. She tells him that he is really responding to a new cancer drug and might be able to go home within the next six to eight months and she wants to stay with him. He tells her to stay if she needs to.

After his nap and it being Friday night, he decides to go out and see what is happening and before he leaves, his phone rings and it's Tommy.

He tells him that somehow the Secret Service has heard something about fake passports coming through the city and they have asked for some help, and I gave them your code name and number and when he asks for Taco, tell him to go ahead and talk.

Sure enough, his phone rings and when he answers, he says, "Taco here, can I help you?" The guy introduces himself as William with the Secret Service, and he understands that he might have some information about some fake passports being moved through the city.

He tells him the story about a guy walking up to him in Jackson Square and giving me a package with several Passports in it and tells me to give the package to the president of the dock board, and he would give me twenty-five thousand dollars in cash, and he gave the package to Tommy.

Then he tells him that since he had gotten hurt, he wasn't going to get too involved with too much stuff but if he happens to hear anything, he will be sure and let him know.

With the weather warming up, he decides to take a bus to Biloxi again and hang around the beach and possibly give Daniel a call and see what he knows about the drugs and the transportation business in Mississippi and for some reason he has had the number thirty-seven in his mind for the last few days.

Chapter 2
Biloxi

When he gets there, he decides to check out the newest Casino there, The Big Dice. It has been open only about six months, and he has heard some really nice things about it.

As he is walking through town headed to the casino, a truck stops beside him at the red light and when he checks it out, there it is, the number thirty-seven on the door. As it drives off, he notices the same number on the license plate.

He checks in the hotel and decides to get himself a bite to eat and then maybe take a nap before he does any checking things out.

When he wakes up and checks his phone, it is two thirty-seven. He showers and looks out the window at the beach and the waves rolling in and thinks, "This just might be a good relaxing trip, and I hope no one decides to mess his trip up and he decides not to call Daniel after all."

After his stroll on the beach, he realizes that he is probably three miles from his hotel and now he must walk back and which does not sound too good at the time. Now what?

He walks up to the highway and sits on a bench, and calls a cab. The cab picks him up and drops him off at his hotel and he is tired and wants another shower to get the beach sand off. As the cab drives off he sees that its number is thirty-seven.

After his shower, he heads to the casino to check things out and possibly play some Texas Hold Um. In the past, he has had winnings on the crap table but for some reason, Texas Hold Um isn't his game, but he thinks he will give it a try.

Six hours later, he decides that he has played enough, and he just might head up to his room. When he gets up from the table, he counts his chips, and he has lost three hundred dollars. Not too bad for playing six hours and before cashing in, he walks over to the Roulette table and puts a hundred-dollar chip on number thirty-seven, and it comes up sixteen and as he is walking away minus a hundred dollars, he turns back around and puts another hundred-dollar chip on thirty-seven, and it hits. Won thirty-six hundred dollars. Cashes in and goes to bed.

Sleeps until noon and showers and walks over to the other casino where he and Spike had met Daniel, the DEA agent. As he goes in the pool parlor, he sees Daniel shooting pool with a group of guys and does not acknowledge him and neither does Daniel acknowledge him.

Pool being one of his better games, when someone invites him to join in, he always does and if he needs to lose to set a trap for someone, he can do that.

Daniel is playing with a group of guys and asks him if he wants to join in and he tells them yes, he would be glad to. As they are playing and talking about who is from where and what they do, one of the guys asks him, "What was he and where was he from?"

He tells them, "I had just served fifteen years in the Nevada state pen for running drugs between Las Vegas and Hollywood and visiting my grandmother in Mississippi." One guy was running from the law, one had been in jail. One was an oilfield worker and Daniel said that he was planning on joining the service.

The longer they played, the more he learned about the other two guys. He says to himself, "Now I am not going to get hooked up with these bad guys, I will let Daniel do that."

The guy who claimed he was on the run from the law finally speaks up.

"I jumped bail in New Orleans for attempted robbery of a C-store… and now here I am, working at one across the street."

Knowing all the bonds people in the city, Lloyd thinks, "Well, I just might get myself some brownie points when I get back. It never hurts to do your friend a favor now and then, he is thinking."

Before long, he and Daniel are taking the other two guys in some money games. The other guys are pretty good until their beer and Vodka take over.

When they completely run out of money, the oilfield worker says, "My brother is doing some drug running here on the coast, and if you guys need anything, I can get it for you. Since I am out of money, I will get you some in place of money."

They both tell him, "No thanks. But how about meeting again tomorrow—maybe you can win your money back?" Lloyd and Daniel play for a while longer until Daniel says, "I better get out of here. Might do a little checking around. See you tomorrow."

Now he must stay over another night and probably give some of his thirty-seven hundred monies back to the casino. Then he says to himself, at the poker room, I really passed the time away and only lost three hundred dollars, so I guess I will go over there and give it another try.

He gets him a snack and goes to the poker room, where he had to wait a few minutes for a space to open. No problem, he thinks, maybe this is a good sign, or maybe it is a bad sign.

Before he knew it, it was three o'clock in the morning, and he was tired. When he cashes out his chips, he sees that he has lost eight hundred dollars. As he is walking to his room, he sticks five dollars in a slot machine and wins a hundred dollars. "All is not lost," he says.

He gets up at ten and goes and gets him some breakfast and happens to see a book he has been looking for in the gift shop. He goes in and buys it and goes outside to the pool area and sits under a canopy out of the sun.

Before he knows it, his phone beeps, and it's Daniel. He heads to the pool parlor and their two newest best friends are waiting for them. They had already planned to let the two bad guys win and then talk some drug trash with them.

After a few games and the bad guys have won a couple of hundred dollars and really think they are some big shot hustlers. Before they got too deep in the alcohol, Daniel says, "Let's go out by the pool and talk about some business before I go in the army, because I would like to have a source of candy while I am working for Uncle Sam."

Buck, the oil field guy, leans in and says, "My brother and sister can get any type of drugs you want. Fast." Clyde the C store bond jumper says, "Hey, I don't know anything about that stuff, nor have I ever been involved with them so I am out of here."

Daniel asks Buck how was it so easy for him to get candy when the DEA is everywhere? He tells them that his brother and sister work for the state and they nearly have free run up and down the highways.

Lloyd asks him what department and he tells him the Transportation department. Bingo! New Orleans dock board, package delivered to Biloxi, Daniel is loving every second of this.

Daniel asks Buck why he doesn't work for the state. He tells him that he is a felon because of something stupid he did when he was a kid, and they won't hire felons, and that is why he works in the oilfields and it is not a bad job. He also added that, "I work fourteen days on and then I am off for fourteen days, and if I ever need money, I can get it from my brother or sister."

Lloyd asks him, "Did he know anyone in New Orleans?" He tells him that he has met a Mr. Donovan who works for the dock board a few times. "How did you meet him?" Daniel asks, and he says that he had delivered and picked up packages from his office and sometimes at a coffee shop on Canal Street.

Lloyd asks him, "Does he have any idea what is in the packages?" and Buck says, "I don't really know but they have something to do with my brother's drug business and I have never asked but I know one thing, whatever they are doing must really pay well because both have bought a house on the beach in Panama City."

Daniel tells Buck that he is too smart to get caught up in the drug business and just keep working in the oilfield and to save his money because when he gets out of the Army, he is going to be a stockbroker and help him make a lot of money.

Then Buck tells them, "I better get going. I'll be gone for two weeks starting tomorrow, but I might see y'all when I get back."

After he leaves, Lloyd tells Daniel, "I don't want to be involved any deeper than I already am. Good luck." He calls a cab and goes to the bus station, and then back to the city.

When he gets home, he checks his mail and decides just to stay in for a couple of days and do nothing and when he gets hungry, walk around the corner, and get a bologna turnover and call it a day.

After a couple of days in his apartment, he gets the urge to check out the streets and the first person he sees is Lester. Lester looks surprised and says, "Man, everybody in the Quarter thought you got killed over in Texas. People were really upset."

He tells him that he had just gone over to the coast for a few days, and he was alive and well and he says that he sure is glad to see him.

The next morning, he gets a call from the chief of police and he asks him, "Can you come by his office for a minute?" He agrees to and heads to the police headquarters on Broad Street.

Everyone is glad to see him, and a lot of the guys gave him a hard time for disappearing and not letting them know where he was going and how long he would be gone.

As he goes up to where the chief's office is, his secretary starts a conversation with him because she has always liked him and has offered to take him to dinner several times. This time, he takes her up on her offer and tells her that he will talk to her after he sees what the chief wants.

As he walks into his office, the chief gets up and closes the door and he is thinking, this must really be important. Then the chief says, "We have a guy that is well known in the community that has come up missing, and we are not telling the public about it currently, and we only know very little about any of this."

"He is David Cole, who owns most all the beauty shops here and in Baton Rouge. His sister came to us asking for help in trying to find him. He has not been to his main shop and office in three days and that is not like him, and he is not at home and his sports car is in his garage."

As the chief is telling him this, he knows the shop manager and a couple of operators and the manicurist. He is thinking, here he should tell Daniel that he doesn't want to get involved in anything and then the chief hits me with this.

Knowing that this could be big city stuff and everyone is always looking after him, he thinks, I just might better get involved and see if I can be of some help.

As he is leaving, Nancy the secretary asks him, "When and where are we going to dinner?" He tells her that he does not have a car, and maybe they should just have dinner in the Quarter. She tells him that she has a car and would be glad to pick him up.

He asks her about Charlie's uptown, and he can take the streetcar and meet her there. She tells him that it would be great because she lives uptown, and how about seven. He agrees and hits the streets.

Now to the missing guy he thinks, with him exposed to all these women, he just might have decided to take one on a short vacation and not tell anyone, or he just might have decided to mess with the wrong lady and get his butt in trouble.

He decides to go to his main shop and get a haircut and see what he can learn and then tomorrow go and get a manicure and this way he might be able to get two different thoughts from the ladies.

As he is getting his haircut, Betsy is whispering in his ear that everyone in the shop thinks he has been seeing a lady who is possibly a part of the underworld families in the area, and if that is true, his ass may be in big trouble. He agrees.

She then tells him that one of the family members always comes in on Wednesday at one o'clock to get her hair done and he is always the one who does her hair. Last week, he told us that he had to go to Baton Rouge on Wednesday to take care of something at his main shop there and the regular Wednesday lady did not come in. She came in on Thursday.

Now with a dinner date, he checks and sees what he has that is halfway decent to wear to the steak house. All he really has is just regular casual, what he calls a poor man's wardrobe.

He goes to Rick's Men's store and sees a guy that he knows and tells him that he must meet some people for dinner at Charlie's and he needs a decent shirt that does not smell like it just came off the rack.

After looking at several fancy shirts and then he gets to what he calls the poor man's rack, he finds one that he likes, and the salesperson tells him to come back in thirty minutes and he will steam it and it won't smell new.

He picks up his shirt and as he is walking back to his apartment, he sees Lester, and he wants him to buy him lunch. At lunch, Lester tells him that the streets are saying that there are some big-time drug dealings somewhere around the docks.

Once again, he is thinking, Spike is ok and wonder just how big the dock thing is for it to get out on the streets and that he is not really tuned into the DEA here in the city for some reason but will see what he can do since he said that he was not going to get involved.

Now that he had picked up his shirt, he goes back to his apartment for a nap. Before he gets down, he calls Tommy and asks him to meet him in the morning for breakfast at nine. He did not have to tell him where to meet. If the time is on the hour, it means the coffee shop is on Canal and if it is on the half hour, it is in the Quarter.

As he is putting on his new shirt and getting ready for dinner with Nancy, he thinks, this is really the first dinner with a lady since he and Mattie broke up over a year ago. Oddly enough, he is looking forward to a little quiet time and a nice dinner. He hasn't been to Charlie's in a couple or three years.

When he and Nancy go in, the waiter knows who he is and puts them in a quiet corner where no one can hear them talking.

They had a lovely dinner and when the waiter told them that they would be closing in thirty minutes, he had no idea how long they had been talking and he had really enjoyed his time with Nancy.

She drives him to his apartment and as he is getting out, she says, "Hey, let's do this again sometime real soon." He says, "It sounds good, and I really enjoyed my evening with you."

He meets Tommy at nine and he tells him that there really must be some big drug dealings going on in and around the dock area for Lester to hear about it. Then he tells him that he really does not know any of the DEA people here or in Baton Rouge.

Tommy tells him that it is because the director over this area is a do-nothing person, and he is afraid that he might have to arrest some big-name person here or in Baton Rouge like the governor or something like that. He likes to get a lot of little guys and not any big fish, as they are referred to.

Then he tells him that there is paperwork in the system to get him transferred to downtown Oakland. That should wake him up and get him off his butt.

When he and Tommy go their separate ways, he decides to go and get a manicure.

Ruth, the manicurist whispers to him saying, "Do you have any idea what the deal is?" He tells her that he does not have any idea and that it may be too early to tell. Then she tells him that yesterday, a guy that none of us have ever seen came in a just looked around and when the girl at the front station asked him if he wanted a haircut, he said no, that he was looking for his cousin.

She then tells him that when this one special lady came in for her appointment with him, there was an awful lot of whispering going on and some close contact. He even walks to her car when he is finished fixing her ugly hair and she drives a Bentley.

When he gets through, he takes a walk to Jackson Square and gives the police chief a call. He gets Nancy and they discuss dinner and then she puts him through to the chief.

He then tells the chief that David was the hairdresser for a lady who they thought may have been related somehow to the underworld figures and they seemed to have a special relationship when he was doing her hair. The people working in his shop had noticed a lot of whispering, laughing, and touching while he was doing her hair and when he finished, he would walk her out to her car.

They cover a lot of what-ifs and maybe that could help put this thing together and see if they can't try and locate David. There has been nothing about any female missing from the city.

Lloyd tells the chief to put out a BOLO (Be on lookout) for any Bentley cars that the police see and to run the plates to see where and who it might be registered to and if they see one, get the info back to the chief as soon as possible.

He brings Tommy up to date so that he can put the word out to the people on the streets to let them know if they just might happen to see a Bentley driving around. They both agree you can't have too many eyes on the streets.

Lester calls him and tells him that they have just discovered a body in the river right by the ferry landing and they are trying to get it out now. He thinks we might have found David, and he will wait until the corner does his thing and then check and see if a tall blond muscle type guy is and if not, who could it be.

As he is heading to his apartment, he says to himself, "Maybe I should move to some place like Sedona, Arizona, or Key West to get away from all this stuff. This is getting to me," he says to himself, "Now Nancy has come into the picture."

The next morning, he walks down to the Corner's office to find out who the body was and that they had fished it out of the river. Since they all know him, he walks right in and asks one of the guys working there did they happened to know who the body was and whether it was male or female.

The guy working in the office tells him that he is a foreigner and must have fallen overboard off one of the freighters in the river. He has nothing in his pockets and looks Asian.

Well, that settles that he says to himself as he leaves to go and get some lunch. He calls Nancy and asks her if she wants to meet him at the Pie Shop for a sandwich and a piece of Key Lime pie. She replies in a millisecond, "Yes, I am on my way."

As they are having lunch, his phone rings and he sees that it is the police chief and as soon as he answers, he says, Yes, she is with me, and do you need to talk to her?" As he is saying that, she is looking at her watch and says, "oh no, I have been gone an hour and a half and she is up and gone saying, call me later."

The chief says, "Since she was late for lunch, I thought she might be with you, and tell her not to rush back." He says, "She is probably in the elevator going up to your office as we speak."

After that little bit of laughter, the chief tells him that so far, they have located two Bentleys in the state. One is registered to an NFL player and the other is to an entertainer from Dallas who is playing at a casino in Biloxi.

Tommy calls him and tells him that his wish has been granted. The local DEA guy is being moved to Detroit and the new director is a female who was born and raised in Houma and from what else he is hearing; she is by the book and a no-nonsense person. Her name is Callie Thibodeaux, and she is being transferred here from New York City and was the DEA director of one of the major airports in the city.

He says to himself, "I bet Daniel will be glad to hear that if he is in her district and if not, oh well it was a thought."

One of the local TV stations has just found out about her coming to the city and are saying that as soon as she gets here that they will try and be the first one to interview her. They all call her a local girl because she was born in Houma, thirty-five miles away and at one time, she was being considered to being nominated by the president to be the national director of the DEA.

As he is walking back to his apartment, he is thinking to himself, "I wonder what the dock workers think about this news story."

He gets one of his books that he has tried to finish for a month and goes and sits in the patio behind Pete's place. It is quiet and the sun only hits it a few hours each day and no one bothers him. Sometime when he is reading, he turns his phone off and hopes the world can get by without him not answering it for a couple of hours.

After two hours of reading, he decides to check and see how many people have called him offering his life insurance at a discounted rate, an extended warranty on a car that he sold two years ago, and special financing when he gets ready to buy his next house.

The only one was a call from Mattie and he called her back. She tells him that her little boy is doing good, and she has some other good news. He tells her, with the news about Booger, what else could be good news.

She tells him that her ex-husband has been there with her and Booger and that he has quit drinking and smoking and has a really good job, and he wants Booger and me to come home and have a real family life. He says, It is great news and for her to tell Rex, if he messes up and hurts either one of you, I will be his worst enemy."

He heard what he had said and said out loud, "Lloyd, you don't ever have to worry about that again, and all I want is to have my family back." "Sounds good," Lloyd says, and "good luck."

Now that David has been missing for a week, things are starting to get a bit more interesting. His brother came in and taken over running the shop in the city and his wife has gone to Baton Rouge to run those parlors. Between both towns, he has nine different shops and is doing a big business and luckily enough, his brother could write and sign checks and pay all of his employees.

His brother had helped get him started with a cash loan from his drug business and was he only relative living other than some cousins and distant aunts and uncles.

Then the TV stations are hitting the air with a missing person report. Mrs. Ellen Porter, the young wife of deceased underworld drug king Richard Porter, has been missing for at least a week. She was last seen leaving home by her maid and she went to her hairdresser and then across the river to the farmers market to buy fresh vegetables.

There will be a news release at tonight's six o'clock tonight by the local police and federal offices about the usual stuff going on. If anyone has seen a green Bentley automobile with plate number 12186, please contact your nearest official police or federal office.

With all that happening, he decides to take his motorcycle and his backpack and ride over to San Antonio to visit his best friend from high school. He enjoys the ride, but it takes all day.

He and his friend just hang out and do nothing. Go to the Alamo and spend some time on the River Walk. Have lunch at the Tower of the Americas and head back to his friend's house, where the walls seem to be closing in on him and he is thinking, "I am out of here the first thing in the morning."

The next morning, he is on the road and decides to split his trip up and not go straight thru back to New Orleans. He makes a detour to Natchitoches, Louisiana. He has been there before and really likes the town and just walking along the river and having some good meat pies.

The next morning, he heads back to the city and is ready to sleep in his own bed. When he stops for fuel, he gives Nancy a call and asks her if she would like a light dinner before he shuts it down for the night.

This way, he can find out what has been going on in the city since he has been gone.

They meet and she brings him up to date. She tells him that everyone is really interested in Ms. Porter being missing and now some people think she might have run away with her hairdresser and the other news is that the African American preacher from the Holy Spirit church passed away and there will be a big funeral in town tomorrow and they are expecting a couple of thousand people to be in the death march to the cemetery.

He is usually in the death marches because he really likes the music and he has made a lot of friends doing that but if there are going to be that many people, he will just stand watch.

The next morning, he is up early and walks over to Mother's for his usual breakfast of ham and eggs and toast. He must get there early because it has the best breakfast in town, and it is always busy. Then he stops by and visits a few friends at the Pearl restaurant and then over to the Sheraton hotel to talk to one of his old running buddies, the bell Capitan.

He hears the music from the death march coming down St. Charles Avenue, headed to Bourbon Street and then onto the Coliseum, where the service will be and then to St. Peter's cemetery then all the dancing and music as they head back into the city.

There are so many people on Canal Street, it looks like carnival time. Sure enough, here they all come dancing, singing, waving their decorated umbrellas and really having a great time.

Nancy calls and tells him, " I think they have found Ms. Porters Bentley in an abandoned storage building behind the old space building in New Orleans east."

A little while later, she calls him again and tells him that it is her car and there are two decomposed bodies inside and once the coroner can be sure who they are, they will have a press conference.

For some reason, all along he has had the thought in his mind that when they find her, and will also find David the hairdresser. He also has a thought in the back of his mind, David's brother is not the most upstanding citizen in the city by just what some of his operators have told him over the past few years.

He does know that his brother did help him get started with some of his drug money, and David's ex-wife had told him a few years ago when they divorced. He had to pay alimony on a sliding scale. As his income went up, his alimony did also and if he dies, she will get half of his business.

It takes all day for any news to come out on finding the Bentley and who the two bodies are that were in it. He says to himself, even I could tell you who they are, and they were probably shot, and someone drove the car there, hoping no one would find them for years. But, oops, that did not happen.

He calls Betsy the girl who cuts his hair and asks, "Did David's ex-wife ever came to the main shop where he was? She tells him that she had not seen her for at least a couple of years but that she was in here yesterday talking to his brother. He asks her, "Was his brother married?" She told him, "She did not know."

Nancy calls him and says, "Hey, let's have dinner." He knew that she would have some news that would not be put on TV yet.

They meet in the Quarter at the coffee shop and get sandwiches and coffee to go and then sit on a bench in Jackson Square away from everyone.

She tells him that they are sure that is Ms. Porter and David and that both bodies were in the front seat pushed all the way against the passenger door like some had killed them, pushed the driver over and then drove the car to the old storage area and that the bodies had exploded from all the heat, and it would be impossible to get and DNA from inside the car.

He asks her, "How did they happen to find the car?" She tells him that a lot of homeless people hang around that area and a homeless vet who had been in a war somewhere recognized the death odor and decided to raise up the door, and the rest is history."

As they are finishing their little snack, he says, "This just might be an underworld hit and it could be a possible inside job or a paid job from some independent hit man. Then he says, "We need to find out if his brother and sister get along and if not, one would not be a suspect. But if they are tight, that is another story."

Better call Ruth to get a manicure and toe job and ask some questions.

He goes to see Ruth and asks her if David's brother and sister were on friendly terms, and she says, "No way. They are like cats and dogs. She is married to a local dentist and lives on the lakefront. His brother is in some kind of junk car and scrap business and is always asking David for a handout and remember, he helped David get started, and I don't know if he gave him a loan or money to get started."

Then she says, "I know one Christmas when David gave all of us a really nice bonus at our party, his brother was there and David said, Hey, everyone this is my brother Carl, and he loaned me five dollars to get started and he is getting a really nice bonus. Everyone laughed and yelled, Thank you Carl."

He takes his time walking back to his apartment and to take a nap and is wondering if Nancy has any vacation time and that he just might ask her to take a few days and go somewhere with him but where does he ask himself?

After his nap and a hot shower, he calls Nancy and asks her if she had any vacation time or days off and would she like to get away for a few days?

She tells him that she has three weeks' vacation and twenty personal days in the bank. Then she says, in other words, we could be gone for a long time or until our money runs out.

Chapter 3
Key West

As they are talking, Miami Beach and Key West pop into his mind. Then he says, "How about Miami Beach for a few days and then drive down to Key West for a few days." She says, "When do we leave and all I must do is let the chief know when I will be leaving and when I might be back."

He goes and finds Lester and tells him that he will be going out of town for about ten days, and he wants him to stay in his apartment to keep the bad guys away.

They make plans to leave next Saturday and be gone for the full ten days. She can hardly wait to get away and to be with him when there is no one around who knows either of them. Every time they try and eat, someone is always wanting to talk to him about something that they had heard, and did he know anything about it?

Four days after they discover the bodies of Ms. Ponder and David, they have a news conference. The police chief tells everyone that they have confirmed the stories about who the deceased are. He also says, "both suffered gunshots to the head and then someone had driven her car to the storage shed, and that is all we know at this time, and they are still trying to collect DNA from her car and the bodies were in such bad shape, they were cremated after the autopsies."

When he stops the news conference he says, "Ms. Ponder's niece claimed her ashes and at this time, no one has claimed David's."

Lloyd keeps saying to himself, his brother did this or had someone do it for him, and in time, the streets will talk, and they are usually right.

The closer it gets to their Saturday trip, the more he is looking for to it. He goes and finds Lester and tells him to try and get to know some of the homeless people around the storage where they found the bodies and if he has to tip them, there is some money in a jar in the freezer. You can use some of the money for cab rides or tips for your friends with a car. Just keep up with how much you spend and what you used it for, he tells him.

Nancy picks him up and they head out to the airport and on to Miami. She is so excited that she is talking ninety miles an hour and nearly driving that fast. She has never been to Florida or even been swimming in the ocean.

He had called ahead and booked a room at a really nice beach hotel with a room overlooking the beach and the ocean. The beachside doors slide open and is just nothing but sunshine and cool ocean breezes.

As soon as they check in, she wants to go swimming and he says, "Ok, let's go get wet." As soon as she runs into the surf, a wave comes in and knocks her down on her butt. When she finally manages to get control of everything, her swim top is half off and one boobs is hanging out and she screams, and he is dying laughing.

It's getting to be the middle of the afternoon and time for his nap. He tells her that it is nap time, and she can stay and play in the water or take a nap also. She tells him that she will go in with him and try to get some of the sand and salt off of her body and then put some lotion on her body and take a nap also.

They have an early dinner and take a long, slow walk on the beach.

The next morning, they are out by the pool early both reading. They both had put sunscreen on to prevent them from getting cooked and possibly ruin their vacation.

For lunch they decided to try out one of the other hotel beach snack areas. As they are eating, some guys walk up and says, "Lloyd Carter what in the world are you doing in Miami Beach with this nice-looking honey beside you?" It's jim Douglas the safety engineer for the oil company that he was working for when his back was broken.

He tells Jim that they are on their honeymoon and having a really good time. Nancy does not know what to say when Jim congratulates her. They visit for a while, and then Jim moves on. Nancy starts laughing and cannot stop. Then she tells him that she nearly fell off her seat when you said that you were on your honeymoon.

The next day, they pack up and drive to Key West. Nancy just cannot get over the beautiful drive down through the keys. They stop a couple of times just to check out things and then move on.

Since neither had ever been to the Keys, it was a new experience for them. They find their hotel and unpack and walk out their door right onto the beach. They are both impressed with the beauty and the ability to just walk out of your room and be on the beachfront.

As he is taking a little nap in one of the lounge chairs, his phone beeps, and he sees that it is Lester.

Lester starts by telling him that about a week or ten days before they found the car and the bodies, some of the guys around there saw a guy just walking around and opening some of the doors on the vacant units where some of them lived.

They all said what he looked like and that he had a funny walk to him. Like maybe he was down in his back or something like that and then he was back a few days later wearing an Indian's ball cap.

Then he told him that one of the homeless guys, who is really a kook and sees ghosts all of the time said that he thinks he heard or saw a car drive in the area, and he thought it might be the police looking for him. Now he says that this guy has come up with some really strange things, but he has been right a few times, most of the other guys say.

He tells Lester to get one of his friends with a car, to drive through the same area at night and then a couple of days later, go and ask this guy did he hear or see anything and then let me know when I get back home.

Before they know it, it is time to head back to Miami to the airport and fly back home. They both sleep all the way home and when she drops him off at his quarter apartment, she tells him that she is not going to like having to sleep alone in her bed. He says, "Yep, I know what you mean, and I will see you tomorrow."

He goes into his apartment, and Lester has left it spotless and everything was in the exact place it was when he left. He has left him a note saying that he had taken a total of sixty dollars out of the jar, and he can explain what he used it for when he sees him.

They meet up at eleven thirty at night at the coffee shop and Lester brings him up to date on what the streets are saying and the big topic is what they are calling the Big Car case.

He tells him that he and a friend drove thru the storage units around ten o'clock one night real slow and then I went out there two days later and ask kook had he seen anything, and he told me that a couple of nights ago when the moon was full, he saw a green car drive thru real slow and then it left. Lester says that his friend drives a green Ford.

Then he had heard that the people who own the old units are having them bull dozed down and we don't know where at the street people will be able to go and be able to stay out of the weather.

While he wants to stay with Nancy, the streets are in his blood, and he has to work out a happy medium between both.

Nancy is back at work and the chief is really glad to see her with her new tanned body he asks her to call Lloyd and ask him to stop when he has time. She calls him and tells him that the chief would like to see him and before she could say anything else, he tells her that he is on his way. She likes that.

As he walks into her office, he says, "Excuse mam but the chief of police has asked me to come to his office and not to be bothering his hired help." She laughs.

They greet one another and the chief askswhat he has heard since he was back? He goes into the story about a guy with a funny walk wandering around the units and comes back a few days later wearing an Indians ball cap and that a green car had driven thru the area one night.

Then he tells him about him having Lester do the same thing, and it was confirmed that someone had driven through the area one night, but no one saw anyone go into one of the old units.

As they are talking, Lloyd has an idea, and he asks the chief to call down where the Bentley is and see if it has any raindrop spots on it. He does, and it has some. Lloyd says that is why no one saw who parked the car because they were all covered up from the rain and could not see or hear anything, especially that high-dollar car.

The chief tells him that they had recovered one forty caliber slug from his head, and it looks like she was in the middle and when she was shot, the slug went all the way through and stuck in his brain. "Two birds with one stone," Lloyd says.

OK, so now we are looking for a guy with possibly a bad back who wears an Indian's ball cap and owns a forty-caliber gun. "A piece of cake," Lloyd says, and the chief says, "Right Dick Tracey."

The brother and ex-wife have been seen at most all of his parlors on regular occasions, always checking the deposits and payroll vouchers. Never together but always separate times.

He is in his apartment lying in bed thinking how they are going to get the brother and possibly ex-wife involved in something. As he is sleeping a noise outside his door wakes him up and he gets his gun and sits up in his bed waiting. Nothing happened and it must have been some drunk trying to find his hotel. As he lays back down, a thought hits him: let's get an interested buyer for David's business and see where that will go.

He sends the chief a text with his thoughts. How about getting an interested buyer for David's business and just seeing what happens? This kind of film flam usually works because the greedy can't stand not putting something in their pockets that they did not have to work for.

The chief gets with the district attorney and wants to be sure that if we are able to get the bad guys, that it is not entrapment. If he says it is ok, let's put our heads together and put this thing to bed.

They tell the manager of his Quarter shop to try and get in touch with David's brother and tell him that you got a phone call from a man in Shreveport who had heard about the killings and was wondering if the family would like to sell.

In the meantime, Lloyd has gotten in touch with a friend in Shreveport who has made millions of dollars in the oil industry, and all he does is play golf and travel to play golf somewhere new every week.

When he runs the idea past old Louie Small, he says that he would like to help out an old buddy from New Orleans.

David's ex-wife comes to the Quarter shop and asks the manager did she has the keys to David's desk because he had told her that he had a life insurance policy for her if something happened to him and she would like to look for it.

The manager did not know what to do, so she went and got a set of keys that had the shop keys on them, along with about a dozen other keys. It takes his ex a rather long time to find the right key because she is in such a hurry.

She finally finds the one to unlock his desk and she starts going through everything in all the drawers. She does not find an insurance policy but finds a key to a lock box at the State Bank of Louisiana. She knows that the bank will not let her open the box without a court order, but she decides to go to the bank and ask them if he had put her name on the card allowing her to open the box.

She goes to the bank, and the clerk says that she will check. She comes back and says that he had not put her name on the card, but it did have the name of Rex Morgan on it. She says that it is his lawyer friend from Slidell, and she will get in touch with him.

As the investigation goes on, there are a dozen stories about what happened and why and anything else that someone could think of was on the streets.

The district attorney called the chief and told him that he had been contacted by Rex Morgan, an attorney from Slidell and was asking if he could come in and talk with you because he had just received a call from David's ex-wife and that he is the executor of David's estate.

He tells the district attorney to tell him that we would love to talk to him, and just give him thirty minutes' notice before he gets here.

Rex calls the chief and asks if he could possibly meet with him at nine in the morning. He told him, "It will be fine, and I look forward to talking with you." As soon as he hangs up, he tells Nancy to get in touch with Lloyd and to have him here in my office at eight forty-five in the morning.

She calls him and tells him that the chief needs him to be in his office at eight forty-five in the morning to meet with a lawyer from Slidell who is the executor of David's estate. He tells her to pick him up after work, and he will just stay with her tonight, and he can ride in with her in the morning. She loves the idea.

The next morning, the three meet and they bring Rex up to date on what they think want just might have happened and would it be a good idea to check his lock box first without his ex being there and he agrees.

Rex and Lloyd walk over to the bank and open up the lock box, and it must have a hundred thousand dollars of cash in it along with some papers.

They find an insurance policy for his burial, and it shows his ex as the person to take care of his funeral. Lloyd says, "Boy, she isn't going to be happy. They both think it is funny, but now what to do with that amount of cash."

They close up the lock box and go back to the chief's office and make plans for Louie to start the process of buying all of David's salons.

Rex says, "How are we going to get that cash out and what can we do with it so the IRS doesn't find out?"

It took him about thirty seconds to come up with an answer. Lloyd says, "Take it and bundle it up and send it by FedEx special handling and to be signed by only the person that it is shipped to, and use a fake name and address and pay cash when you send it."

"You send it to the CEO of St. Jude in Memphis and hope he is an honest guy.' Then he says, "You can always use a person's name that has just died as the shipper."

Rex says, "Why didn't you go to law school?"

Louie Small, his friend from Shreveport, comes to town to find out a little about the beauty parlors that he is interested in buying. They have lunch together and he brings Louie up to date on what happened and where the bodies were found, and they think it just might be his brother and ex-wife doing the dirty work.

They go to the shop in the Quarter and Louie gets a manicure from Ruth and she tells him everything she knows about how many shops there are and any other thing that a potential might want to know from an employee's eyes.

Then Lloyd takes Louie up to the front and introduces him to Sally, the shop manager. She had worked for David for over ten years and knows a lot about him and his business. They tell her that Louie is in town and would like to find out that, since David had passed away, he was wondering if the family would like to sell him business because he is moving to New Orleans.

They visit a little and she tells them that she will try to get in touch with his brother and pass the word on to him. Louie gives her his business card and tells her to have the guy call him if he is interested in selling all of the shops.

Louie wants to go and play golf since they had gotten their business done and they head out to City Park to play. After they finish playing, they go to the Sheraton hotel on Canal Street and get a massage and spend some time in the sauna and then take a walk around town.

They stay up half the night just doing nothing and their plan for tomorrow is to go and visit the World War Two museum. He stays with Lloyd.

Salley, the salon manager calls him and tells him David's brother had called about coming buy to get the bank deposit and she had told him about Louis asking about him possibly selling and he told her that he would talk to her about it when he stops by.

Lloyd calls Betsy and asks them to watch how the brother walks when he comes in to see Sally. They both laugh and ask why, and he tells them that he will tell them later, and there will be a nice cash reward for them doing it.

As they are touring the museum, his phone beeps, and he goes outside, and it is Ruth. She tells him that his brother had just stopped by and spent a few minutes talking to Salley and that she had walked over to him and told him how sorry she was that we had lost David and if there was anything she could do for him, to just let her know.

As she walks back to her station, she sees him go into the back to the restroom area and then walk out the front door. She thought that he walked like he had a catch in his back and bent over a little.

Then Betsy calls him and says that the brother walked like he had a dime stuck in his butt and a dollar bet that he wouldn't drop it. He drops his phone and says, "Here, tell Louie what you just told me."

He listens and then goes crazy laughing, and he tells her that they owe her dinner for that, and to bring Ruth.

The four of them go to dinner at The Summit Club, where Lloyd is a member. After three hours of them eating and having a few drinks, he finds himself with three drunks and now what does he do? The owner stops by their table and tells them that he will be closing in about thirty minutes and that he just wanted them to know.

Fortunately, both of the girls are single and don't have husbands to go home to drunk. He calls a cab, and they all go to his apartment and the three drunks sleep on the floor with no bedding or pillows.

He lets them sleep until nine and then he starts the process of trying to wake them up and show them where the bathroom is. Both girls were to be at work at eight, and both had appointments. As they are starting to move around, he calls Salley and tells her that the girls are partly alive and should be in a little later, and tells their customers that they were just running late and nothing else.

As they are having lunch, Lloyd's phone rings. It's an attorney named Junior Baker, who says, "My client, Richard Douglas, told me you might be interested in buying David's business. Do you have the funds to possibly make that happen?"

Louis tells him, "Don't worry about whether I have the funds to buy the business—because if I didn't, I wouldn't be wasting my time talking to you."

That shuts the guy up for a moment.

Then Junior asks, "When could we possibly meet to talk?"

Louis replies, "Anytime. That's up to you. But when we meet, I want to see the last three years' P&Ls."

Junior responds, "How about ten o'clock tomorrow morning at my office?"

"We'll see you there," Louis says.

When the call ends, Lloyd shakes his head and tells Louis, "Junior Baker is the world's worst attorney—crooked as a barrel of snakes. He spends more time in front of the state board trying to save his law license than he does in the courtroom."

Lloyd then calls Rex.

"You want to have lunch with Junior Baker tomorrow?" he asks.

Rex immediately bursts into laughter. "Man, I don't even want to be seen in the same restaurant as him. Why are you meeting with that guy?"

After Lloyd explains the situation, Rex chuckles again and says, "Just make sure to wash your hands if you shake his—and burn your clothes after you've been in his office."

Lloyd tells Louie to go by himself because when Junior sees me, he will get nervous and probably wet his pants. Louie asks him why and he tells him that years ago he and two other people saw a mock wreck and when three people jumped into the car that had been hit from the rear, he was their attorney and when myself and the other people testified in court what happened, his clients were arrested for insurance fraud and he has raked over the coals for not really knowing what happened and who he was representing.

Louie goes and sees Junior, and they look at the P& L's for David's business and just really talk, and no money was discussed if he was interested in the business, but Junior was starting to try and pressure Louis to make an offer. He tells Junior that he will want to meet with David's brother and find out just why he wants to sell and just try and get to know the guy.

Then Junior tells him that David's ex-wife might become a problem because she is saying that he had an insurance policy for her if something happened to David, and she wants to find out how much it is worth.

Louie tells him that he will get back with him when he can arrange a meeting with the brother and ex-wife, because if he buys the business, he does not want any surprises or problems at a later date. Junior tells him to trust him, and there won't be any problems at a later date.

Now, Louie and Lloyd go to and see the chief of police and the district attorney and tell then everything that they know and that the brother does have a slightly different walk because one of Lester's homeless friends at the storage building area said that a guy had been seen walking around the area before they found the car and bodies.

The district attorney said that they will need more than that to issue an arrest warrant. They leave the meeting scratching their heads, wondering what to do next.

As they are having lunch, all of a sudden Lloyd stops eating and looks around and says, "Since there have been a few robberies in the Quarter lately, let's have Sally call Richard and ask if he owns a gun. She can tell him the salon handles a lot of cash, especially on Fridays and Saturdays— and she wants something for protection." "Sounds good," Louie says.

Junior calls Louie and tells him that he can have Richard and the ex-wife in his office tomorrow at one o'clock to talk about possibly buying the business, and he tells him that he will see them there.

As they are sitting in Jackson Square checking out the scenery, Lloyd's phone rings and he sees that it is Rex. When he answers, Rex tells him that he hopes he does not get in trouble, but he has just sent a package by FedEx to Memphis using a guy's name that died last week, and his ashes were buried yesterday.

Then he tells him that he walked five blocks to the FedEx shipping office and even wore a disguise so no one would recognize me. Now his ex can get into the lock box because I gave the bank a written letter allowing anyone to get access to the box.

They tell Sally to give Richard a call about one fifteen while they are in Junior's office, and tell him the gun story and that they will see if Louie can pick up on anything.

Right on time, Richard and the ex-wife arrive at Junior's office, and right behind them is Louie. Before anything is said, the ex tells Junior that David had an insurance policy for her if something happened to him, and she knows that it is in a lock box at the Louisiana bank, and probably Rex Morgan can get in the box.

Junior says, "I know Rex, and I will give him a quick call and see what he has to say." He does and Rex tells him that he has given the bank permission to let anyone open the box who wants to. Junior thanks him and says, "Why don't we do lunch one day when you are in town and hangs up."

He tells the ex-wife, "You can go and access the lockbox anytime."Just as they are about to start the meeting, Richard's phone rings and he says, "Hello Sally, how are you doing today?" He listens and after a couple of minutes, he says, "You know, you are right, and that is a good idea, and I actually have a couple and one in my car." Then he says, "Do you know how to use one?" and he laughs and tells her that he will drop by the salon after he gets through with this meeting.

Then Louis says, Let's get serious about a possible big-time business deal getting done. As they are talking, Louie realizes that David had one really profitable business, not counting the cash business that they put in their pockets.

In his mind, he thinks, "I just might get serious about this business, but first, the cat has to catch the mouse." Then he turns to Richard. "Now, with David gone, that obviously affects the value of the business. I'd need to review everything before I could make an offer, if that's okay with you."

"Sounds good," Richard replies. "When do you think you'll be ready?" "Give me a couple of days. I need to talk to my CPA," Louie says. Then he turns to the ex-wife. "Do you have any involvement in the sale of the business?" She shakes her head. "No. I'm only here because of the insurance policy."

They all agree to meet again on Thursday afternoon at three to continue the conversation.

Later, Sally calls Lloyd and tells him that she has the gun, and he calls the chief and tells him. The chief sends the crime investigation team to the shop so they can test fire the gun to see if the slug matches the slug found in David's brain.

As Lloyd and Louie talk, Louie says, "That business David had—it was solid. A real moneymaker. And that's not even counting the cash they never reported." Then he says, "You sell the four in Baton Rouge to the employees and keep the five good ones here in the city. Then maybe we could find you a wife out of all the females that come thru the doors.

Lloyd tells him, "She'll never come through those doors."Then he thinks about Nancy and the good times he always has when he is with her. But that can wait.

Just then, Nancy calls from the chief's office.

"The chief wants to see you both as soon as possible," she says.

"We're on our way," Lloyd replies.

As they walk toward police headquarters, Louie says, "If the slug matches and they arrest him, they'd better search the ex's house too—just to be sure."

They get to the chief's office, and Nancy shows them in. There are a couple of other people in his office, and he thinks, now what is this, going to be something serious or a dog and pony show.

The chief introduces one guy as the director of the crime lab, and the other guy is the new assistant district attorney. The director of the crime lab says, "The bullet fired from the gun this morning that was at the beauty parlor is the same gun that fired the fatal bullet that was recovered from David Douglas's brain."

The assistant district attorney says, "Do you guys have any other ideas that we should look into before we issue arrest warrants?" Louie says that he would do a complete search of his house and his ex-wife's house also and at the same time. They all agree that they will arrest both of them on Thursday at Junior's office and start the searches at the same time, and then have someone pick up the gun from the beauty shop.

They also decide to do a fake arrest of Louie to make it a little more dramatic.

Thursday finally gets there, and Lloyd is nervous for some reason, and Louie is excited about what he is calling the cops and killers meeting.

As the four of them are in Junior's office, the police come in and say, "We are looking for Richard Douglas and Mary Douglas, and Louie Small." When they all identify themselves and the police tell them all to stand and to put their hands behind their backs Junior says, "Whatever they did, I did not have anything to do with it."

They read each one their merenda rights and separated them, and put each one in a separate car. Louis says, once you get these cuffs on, the funny part goes away.

While he a Lloyd are talking about what and how everything went down, Nancy calls and tell them that found a set of Bentley car keys in Mary Douglas' house and Richard's house, they found a pair of sneakers with the same type of mud on them as the same kind as it is at the old storage units.

Louie tells Lloyd that he has had about all the fun he can stand for a while, and he is going home, and to keep him informed on how everything turns out, and that he is interested in buying David's business. Lloyd asks him, "Who is he going to buy it from?"

Chapter 4
A New Day

He goes to his apartment and takes a hot shower, and goes to bed, saying to himself, "This isn't going to happen to me again, and that is a fact."

As he wakes up, he looks at his clock and it shows one forty-five a m. He gets up, dresses and hits the streets. He says to himself, "This is life."

He walks over to the all-night coffee house and sees a lot of his regular friends, and everyone asks him where he has been. His basic answer is, "You don't want to know and if I told you, you would not believe me."

As the sun tries to break thru the morning fog, he just sits and thinks how nice it is to be able just to sit and relax when other people are bitching about the morning fog. Along with the fog, there are the Quarter sounds of the city waking up and things starting to happen.

Street sweepers are trying to clean up everything from all the drunks last night, the garbage trucks making their runs and the natives washing off their steps where the haints sat last night.

Even in today's modern times, the old families still wash off their stoop, as they call it, because sometime during the night, the haints, whatever that is just happened to stop by and sit on theirs, and they get their hose pipe and clean them off and then clean the banket.

As he is headed to Mother's to get some breakfast, he sees Lester leaning up against a light pole in the middle of the streetcar tracks. He goes over and asks him, "What's the matter?" and tells him that he is really hurting in his chest, and it is hard for him to breathe.

He dials nine one one and tells the operator that Lester must be having a heart attack, and the operator knows who he is and says that she will get EMS rolling. He stays with him until the rescue people get him loaded up, and he is off to the hospital.

As he is walking, he says to himself, "Now God, please don't let anything happen to Lester. I know he is a good person, but please don't take him home just yet."

After his breakfast, he walks to General Hospital to check on Lester. Since everyone knows him, he has the freedom to move around the E.R. When he finds him, the doctor tells him that he has a heart problem and will have to have a heart Cath before long and that he needs a couple of weeks' bed rest and some decent food.

He tells the doctor that he will move him into his apartment and will be sure that he rests and gets some decent food.

Then the doctor says, "I know you walk around these streets all day and night, but after your two weeks' bed rest, I want you to walk at least thirty minutes every day without stopping. Now don't walk ten and rest. That is thirty minutes at once, and then we are going to get you walking up to two hours every day because African Americans can developer heart problems quicker than other races of people. Do you understand?"

As he is walking back from the hospital, he decides to give Nancy a little visit and ask her if she would mind if he stayed with her for a couple of weeks while Lester is on the mend.

When he asks her, she nearly jumps out of her chair, telling him, "Yes, you're more than welcome." She gave him a key to her place.

Lester is finally released, and he takes him to his apartment and gives him a list of what he can and cannot do, and if he decides to check on him and he is not in the apartment, he will have him shot on sight. Then he tells him that the refrigerator is full of the right kind of food, and for breakfast every morning, he wants him to eat at least three eggs and some orange juice, and no beer or soft drinks, and he damn sure not better light up a smoke in his apartment. Lester tells him that he hasn't smoked in thirty years.

After a couple of nights, while Lester is in his apartment, he goes and sleeps on the floor just to be able to walk the streets at night and keep abreast of what's happening. Nancy understands.

When the two weeks are up, he decides to let him stay a couple more weeks, but he has to start his walking program today, and he is going to walk with him.

They start walking and Lester brings him up to date on his past and where he was from. He tells him that he was born and raised close by area and that his mother was a schoolteacher, and his daddy was a preacher, and they were both killed in a car wreck while he was in Southeast Asia.

Lloyd nearly falls, not knowing that he had been in the Vietnam War and was a veteran. He knew that he had gone in the military to keep from going to the state pen. After hearing that, he really didn't remember what else he said, and Lester says, "Hey, we have been walking for an hour and ten minutes. Does this mean that I don't have to walk tomorrow?" He tells him no, and now they have to walk back into town.

They were nearly three miles from his apartment. As they start back, Lester picks up again from where he stopped. He told him that he had served three tours in the war and was fortunate not to get killed or seriously wounded, and he lost a lot of friends over there and was told that he was suffering from PTSD and that is why he couldn't hold a job and he somehow ended up living off the streets.

Lloyd says, "My man, we are going to keep walking, and we are going to the V.A. office in the federal building, and you are going to be taken care of."

They get to the V A office and take a number, and wait for their turn. They call his number, and they go and sit in front of this very attractive African American lady, and she introduces herself as Miss Taylor and asks, "What can I do for this fine-looking pair of guys?"

Lloyd says, "Now Lester, don't get your hopes up." He then tells her that Lester is his best friend and had a little heart trouble a couple of weeks ago, and she interrupts and says, "A little heart trouble, there is no truth to a little heart trouble." They all laugh. Then he tells her, as they were walking, he just happened to say, while he was in Southeast Asia, that his parents were killed in an automobile accident, and as long as he had known him, he had no idea that he was a veteran. He was told that he had PTSD and had been living on the streets for God only knows how many years.

She asks him for his social security number, and when she pulls up his file, her face gets a small frown and then a smile and then another frown and then the first thing she asks him, "Where are all of your medals?" He tells her that all of his military stuff was stolen years back and that he did not know how to go about getting them replaced.

After reading more about his service, she says, "Excuse me for a minute, and I will be right back."

They just sit there not talking, and a little later she comes back and says, "Sargent Parker, come with me and friend, just sit there and wait, and I will talk to you later." She takes him by the hand, and they go off into the back offices.

After a bit, she comes back and sits at her desk and says, "I am sorry, but I didn't get your name." He tells her that he goes by Lloyd.

Then she says, "Well, brother Lloyd, your friend Sargent Lester Parker is one of the most decorated soldiers to come out of the war and was wounded five different times and was nominated for the Congressional Medal of Honor."

He asked her what she had done with him. She tells him that he is with the main doctor, Major Burks. He is being evaluated for military disability, and his days of being homeless are over if I have anything to say about it.

They sit and talk about everything that is going on in the city, and she asks him, "Did he hear about the guy's brother killing him and Ms. Ponder and putting them in a storage shed?" He said that he had a little about it because he doesn't watch the national or local news.

She asks him why he doesn't watch any news. He tells her that you really don't know what to believe and they very seldom report on anything good. It's always about how bad the economy is, and there was a killing just down the street. She says, "You are right, and it is a shame what is happening in the world today."

After a bit, Lester and Major Burks come walking up. He introduces himself to Lloyd and says, I don't know if you know it or not, you are friends with one hell of a good guy. I am classifying him as one hundred per cent disable, and he will start receiving a monthly check in about ninety days and I am going to put in for the last ten years that he has not received his benefits, and if I can get that approved, he will be well off.

Ms. Taylor asks him what address he will be using, and Lloyd gives her his address. "Does she have any idea how much he will be receiving each month, because he wants to go ahead and get himself a decent place to live?" She tells him that it will be close to four thousand dollars a month.

He has never seen Lester with bright eyes and a smile on his face. He is a totally different person, and when Lloyd says, "Come on, you are buying lunch, he stands and tries to straighten his shirt" and says, "Miss Taylor, can I buy you a steak dinner when I get my first check?" She says, "Mr. Parker, you can buy me a burger, and I would be happy with that."

As they are leaving the federal building, Lester says, "I think we'd better sit down on this bench and just try and figure out what just happened," and he says, "it's because you wanted to walk three miles and nearly killed me."

Lloyd says, "Now you will have enough money to join a health club and build your heart up so that you won't need a heart Cath job, and where do you think you would like to live, and we need to go and buy you some new clothes and shoes." Lloyd says, "I will pay for them, and you will always be in debt to me."

After spending nearly two hours on the bench, Lester says, "You know, I don't want to live in the quarter. If I do, sooner or later, I might get in trouble and must kick some butt and possibly go to jail. How about a small apartment up town close to the university, and maybe I could go to school on the G.I. bill and become an Astronaut."

They agree that he can stay in Lloyd's apartment until he starts getting his money, and by that time they will have found him a place to live. Lloyd will take care of the deposits and possibly get him settled even before he gets his money, and then they go to a local bank and get him an account set up for direct deposit and when that is done, he can take the info to the V A and see Ms. Taylor.

They agree to meet the next morning and get their exercise, and Lloyd says, "Hey, I'm not the one that the doctor told to walk, and why am I walking?" Lester says, "It is because you love me! Right!" He says!

As they are walking, Lester will bring up some of his past military experiences. A lot of stuff about what he and a lot of his army buddies did while in boot camp and on R & R. Very little about his combat experience.

Then he goes back to his childhood and being raised in East Texas. With his daddy being a preacher and his mother a schoolteacher, I had to toe the line when it came to getting in trouble.

In high school, he says, "I was a three-sport kid. Football, Baseball and Track. I know what you are going to say. Why not basketball? Because every African American kid plays basketball. I never liked the game, so I didn't play."

"I was offered several sports scholarships. Mostly football. I was a tight end. Being six foot three and two hundred and forty pounds, I was big for a high school kid."

Being raised in the Church of Christ, everyone said, "I should go to ACU or Harding. Both strict church schools and I knew that was not going to work."

So, with that said, "I wanted to stay in Texas, and I decided to take the offer from SFA. That was a mid-sized four-year college and not too far from home. Not having a car, I had to depend on others to get back and forth to school, and hitchhiked a lot to get back and forth."

When we started the fall practice, I felt great and was looking forward to going to school and playing ball. I had a three point oh GPA and knew that I would do ok and get a degree like my parents wanted me to do.

Once classes started, everything went downhill. For some unknown reason, I just did not feel right on campus or in class. I guess I was having panic attacks and did not know it. I would be sitting in class and break out in a sweat or nearly pee on myself.

After two weeks of pure hell, I asked a friend to take me home so I could talk to my parents and tell them about the troubles I was having, knowing that they would be disappointed in me, but I had to do it.

To my surprise, they both agreed that I was not cut out for college life, and so I decided to go to a Vo Tech school close to home. Really enjoyed it. Took welding, automobile mechanics, plumbing and a couple of other hands-on classes.

With mother being a schoolteacher and daddy being a preacher, we weren't rolling in the cash, but we were comfortable and had a rather nice home.

One night when I was driving home from seeing a girl in the town next to ours, my old car decided just to quit and leave me alongside the road. So, I started walking home like we are doing now. I had walked a couple of miles when two guys stopped and asked me if I could use a ride, and I said yes and thanked them. I got in the back of their truck. Big mistake.

They took off down the road real fast and would slam on the brakes, throwing me all over the back of the truck. Then they would fly around corners, throwing me all over the back. I was thinking, this is a bad way to die.

When they finally slowed down enough that I could jump out, I bailed out and hit the ground hard. That is when they made their first and last mistake.

They walked up to me, and before either one of them could say anything, I knocked the big one out with a fist to his face and then the other one tried to get away. He did not make it.

The next morning, the police came to the house to talk to me. When I got home, I woke my dad up and told him what had happened and showed him all the cuts and scratches I had all over my body.

When we went to the door, one smart ass cop said, "Hey boy, we want to talk to you." My dad said to him, Excuse me sir. That is no way to start a conversation with my son, and could you please start over?" Then he said, "ok pops, I want to talk to Lester."

My mother had heard all of this and had called the local justice of the peace, who we had been friends with all my life and was telling him everything that was going on.

The cop was saying that they were there to arrest him for assault and causing bodily harm. When I tried to explain what had happened, he did not care to hear what I had to say and started to come into our house.

Now my dad was about six foot six and weighed around two hundred and eighty pounds, and this was the first time in my life that I saw him getting mad and when he said, "Son, that is not a good idea for you to put one foot on my step."

About that time, J.P. Mike drove up and asked what was going on. The cop said, "Lester had assaulted two kids, and they want him arrested."

Mike says, "Lester, tell us what happened last night." After he had explained what had happened and showed them all his cuts and scratches, the cop extended his hand and said that he was sorry for being so rude, and it sounded like they got what they deserved.

The next thing I knew, I was in Southeast Asia getting shot at by some little guys that were as mean as snakes. I was thinking, man, these people really must not like black people. They both burst out laughing.

Now they are three miles from where they started. Lloyd says, "Do we walk back or call a cab? We walk, Lester says.

On the way back, Lester tells him that when he got out of the army and did not have a mother or daddy to go home to, he had a cousin down here, and he was with all the family I had and moved down here and lived with them. Now you think Southeast Asia was bad, it was nothing like living with all those crazy, drugged-up relatives.

So, one day when I had sixty dollars in my pocket, I said to myself, "I can do better than this by being homeless, and here I am."

They finally get back to his apartment, and Lloyd says, "Man, I need a nap." Lester says that he is going to the V.A. to give them his banking information and that he will talk to him later.

Nancy calls and wakes him up and asks him what he would like for dinner, and he tells her a foot massage. He tells her that Lester has nearly killed him, and he will be at her house in a little while and order anything except Thai.

At dinner that night, Nancy tells him that the chief will have a news conference tomorrow, bringing the city up to date on the Ponder killings. She says that he is not going to mention anything about how they were able to solve the case, and that it will be left up to the court system, and that both suspects were denied bonds.

As they were talking, he told her about Lester's upbringing and how he ended up in the army and then on the streets. She says, "You really care for him, don't you?" He said, "like a brother that I never had." Then his phone rings and he sees that it is Lester, and when he answers, he says, "Ok, now what have you gotten yourself into?"

He tells him that he is inviting him and Nancy to dinner Friday night with him and Ms. Sissy Taylor at Buster's Hamburgers, and can I borrow a couple of hundred dollars to be sure I can cover the dinner bill?

They make plans to meet and talk tomorrow while getting in their miles of walking and talking. As they are on their daily trip, Lloyd tells him that he needs to get a driver's license so that when he needs a car, he will be ready. Lester tells him that he has not driven a car in probably fifteen years, but I guess it's like riding a bicycle; once you know how, you won't forget.

Lester then tells him about asking Sissy out to dinner, and she said that there was no way that she could refuse dinner with a great army sergeant, and she was looking forward to it. He then tells him that she has never been married and has a degree from LSU in social studies. Lloyd says she will need that to put up with you.

Friday arrives, and they all meet at Buster's and are really enjoying their dinner. Sissy brings them up to date on where she was from and everything in general about work, and just general conversation. Lester is eating it up.

Having been homeless for so long, he had never forgotten his manners and how and when to talk and when to listen. Then Sissy says that after visiting with Lester at her office and everyone trying to listen to what they are saying, she suggests that he write a book about his life's experiences.

Look, she says, "kid from East Texas, ball player, truck ride, Vo Tech, army, homeless, seeing a murderer, and now eating with the big dogs. They all love it." Then she says, "Now I did not tell you this, but your doctor really likes you and is still trying to get your disability back pay for your PTSD, and if that is approved, you could get a ton of money."

You figure it up yourselves. Four thousand dollars a month for one hundred and twenty months is not chicken feed. Lloyd says that he would buy a lot of chickens, and somewhere in the back of his mind he is saying, "This might be too good to be true."

Lester and Sissy head out to walk around the Quarter, and he and Nancy go to her house. Once there, she says, "OK, what's on your mind, big boy?" He says, Oh! nothing really." She says, "Dog don't hunt." Then she says, "Are you thinking the same thing I am?" He says, "Probably so and let's see what the streets have to say."

As they are taking their daily walk, Lester says, "Well, you don't have much to say today, do you?" He tells him that he is wondering why he is doing all this walking, like I said earlier, the doctor told you to walk and not me.

They walk for another thirty minutes, hardly saying anything until Lloyd says, "Ok, big boy, let's sit and have a little street talk." Lester says, "I am ready. What do you have? " he asks.

Lloyd says, "Do you have any idea where I am headed?" Lester says, "I just might have a small idea, so before you start, I will send you one word on your phone, and then we can talk."

Then Lloyd says, "You know that there is a possibility that you could get a ton of money from your back disability, and there are people in this world that would like to share it with a guy that has been homeless for several years and not knowing how to handle a big windfall."

Lester says, "Look at your phone." He does, and there is one word there. Sissy! Then he says, "You know I might have been born in the dark, but it wasn't last night."

Lloyd says, "Let's finish our walk." They talk all the way back into the Quarter, where they decide to get something to eat. With it being Saturday, the restaurants don't usually have a daily special. They go to Johnny's and eat oysters.

Nancy calls and tells him about a nice garage apartment in the uptown area close to the college, and that the people want someone who is reliable and a non-drinker to stay there and do a little yard work and help them out around their house, and the rent is free. Lloyd says that he will take it jokingly.

She gives him their number, and he calls and asks, "Can they come by and see it?" They say, "Come on by, and we will be looking forward to seeing you."

As Lester is walking up their driveway, he sees an Army retired officer's sticker on a car in the driveway. Just as they are about to ring the doorbell, a man opens the door and says, "Hi, I am Dick Arnold, and this is my wife Ruth, and come on in."

They go in and start talking, and then they take them out back to a nice garage apartment. It is up over the garage and looks like it has never been used much. And as they are talking, Lester says, "Mr. Arnold, I see that you are a retired army officer and when and did you serve, and what rank were you when you retired?"

He tells him when, where and what rank he was when he retired. After he tells him everything he had asked about, they figure out that they were in Southeast Asia at the same time, and at one time they were fighting out of the same fire base, and they find out that Dick was a retired general, and the rest is history.

Lester is now living in a garage apartment uptown New Orleans and is planning on taking some college classes. He and Dick will have some good times together.

They decide just to go ahead and walk back into the Quarter and try and figure out what else they can do today. Lester tells him that he does not want or need a car, and he can go ahead and get his license, just in case the Arnolds want me to take them somewhere or go and get something.

Once again, they find themselves sitting on a bench in Jackson Square, talking about stuff as they refer to it. As always, they are people watching and are trying to guess what some people do for a living. Every time they see a guy in a suit and tie, they know that he works at one of the banks in the central business district.

The tourists are always taking pictures and just walking and looking at everything, and then they see one of Lester's old friends trying to hustle a buck for a sandwich.

Now that Covid has somewhat gone away, the street musicians are starting to play in the square area and over by the coffeehouse. No matter how many times they have heard them play, they always enjoy their time listening to them. Lester tells him that one time, a few years ago, he joined up with a bunch and sang a few songs and picked up fifteen dollars.

As they get a little warmth from the sun, they both drop off to sleep a little, and through experience they can both sleep sitting up and not bother the person beside them.

Lester's phone rings, and he sees that it is Mr. Arnold, and he answers his phone saying, "Yes sir general, what can I do for you today?" He laughs and says, "Yes sir and I will get the key later today and water the flowers just in the back area, pick up the newspapers, and you will be back a week from today. Got it and have a safe trip," he says and hangs up.

After that, Lester says, "Excuse me, sir. Now that I have a job, I'm going to take the streetcar to my residence. Have a nice day." He heads off to catch a streetcar and go to his own place for the first time since getting out of the service.

As he is walking with pep in his step, he stops and says to himself, "Thank you, Jesus and thank you for my brother, Lloyd."

With the weekend here, he decides to stay in his apartment so he can keep an eye out to see who is in town and what just might be happening. Most of the time, he just walks the streets that border the quarter. That is usually where the bad guys try and plan their dirty work and when he sees them, they usually break up and move on.

He has a keen eye when new ladies of the night are in town. When he sees them, he usually welcomes them to town, and then he tells them what the fine and jail time is if they get caught hustling. Some of them leave right away, and then some of them test the system.

Now, when it's a bowl game or something like the Super Bowl, he doesn't waste his time trying to keep up with all of them then because there are way too many to count, and he always says, "I guess they need to make a living like everyone else."

Lester sends him a picture of himself with one of the general's caps on, watering the flowers with a note saying life is good.

Rex, his attorney friend from Slidell, calls him and tells him that Louie wants to come down and possibly buying David's salons here in New Orleans because, after looking at the P&Ls, this is a real top-notch money maker and might want to buy them for his daughter and son-in-law.

Then he tells him, since David did not have any kids and there is no will to be found, it will have to go thru the court system, and he is going to get in touch with a judge to ask him if he could get someone in there so that all the operators could be paid and then try to sell off the ones in Baton Rouge.

He tells him that this is not going to be easy, but it can be done.

Two days later, the shop manager from Baton Rouge calls Lloyd and says that all the operators in Baton Rouge want to form a corporation and buy the salons there and asks him to go about it. He gives her Rex's number and wishes her good luck.

Not one to watch a lot of news, when something happens, his phone will beep, and he checks it out to see if the world is coming to an end.

There is a local news break from Biloxi. A TV station has just announced that a big drug ring has been caught, and there are a lot of state officials involved and they are also looking into some of their business dealings with some people from New Orleans. Interesting, he says to himself, and he is glad that he had nothing to do with any of that.

For some reason, he feels like the walls are closing in around him, and he just might get on his bike and take a trip for a few days but where?

He gets in touch with Tommy, his agent friend and says, "Let's have lunch tomorrow." He agrees, and they meet at Buddy's Burgers. Tommy asks about the Ponder murders, and he gives him a blow-by-blow story on how and when and what happened, and they were lucky to solve it in such a short amount of time and one of his homeless friends had some key evidence.

As they are talking, he asks Tommy if he could get on a bike and take off with no place in mind. Where would you go? He tells him that he would go to New Mexico and Arizona, and then into Utah. Now that is a lot of bike time, but it is probably the most beautiful part of the country.

He goes to his apartment and gets his Atlas down, and starts looking at a possible route through the areas that Tommy talked about. After looking at a possible trip route, he thinks he can ride between four and five hundred miles a day if the weather is good.

After checking the milage, he says to himself, "Damn, it will take me three days just to get across Texas."

When he and Nancy are having dinner, he tells her about him possibly taking a bike trip for a few days and checking out an area that he has never seen, and if he likes what he sees, maybe they could take one together sometime.

Knowing how he was, she told him that he would really enjoy the trip and that she would miss him and look forward to seeing him when he got back.

Being the night person that he is, he plans to ride a lot at night and sleep during the day. If he finds some nice camp areas, he just might sleep out in the open.

He goes and sees the police chief and tells him about his plans and that he will be carrying his gun, and he could get him some kind of New Orleans Police I D just in case he is stopped with his gun. The chief gets him a badge and then sends him to the I D department to get his picture made, and now he is a New Orleans policeman.

He gets his bike serviced, buys new tires, and gets his backpack ready with all his personal stuff, and bed roll fixed, saddle bags filled, a quart of extra gas, cash, travelers' checks, two credit cards, and he is ready to go. Lester is to check his apartment and get his mail.

With daylight savings time, it doesn't get dark until nine o'clock, and he waits until about that time. He rides all the way to Dallas and isn't tired at all, so he stops and gets gas and then heads towards Amarillo.

He decides to stop in Decatur, Texas and call it a long day. He sleeps until six thirty and decides to get something to eat and wait for the sun to go down a little more before he gets back on the road. He really feels rested and is not tired after a good sleep and a hot meal.

As the sun is setting, he fires up his bike and hits the road, headed to Albuquerque and then Santa Fe. Gets to Santa Fe around six in the morning and finds a nice motel, and goes to bed. He always brings his bike into the room where he is sleeping, and he had booked the room for two sleep-ins, as he calls it.

He spends the day just walking around the square and checking out all the various shops. He really likes what he sees. He has always been a big supporter of the Native Americans and their culture.

The next day, he checks out Angel Fire, Taos, and Eagle's Nest. He loves the mountains. Before he knows it, the sun is setting, and he does not want to be on the mountain roads at night. He makes it in and goes to bed.

The next day, he rides from Albuquerque to Sedona, Arizona through Oak Creek Canyon. He thinks to himself that it must be one of the prettiest drives in the country. He books a room for a couple of nights and then rides up to Jerome, Arizona. An old mining ghost town on top of a mountain.

After a couple of days there, and rides to the south rim of the Grand Canyon. He is lucky to be able to get a room at the world famous El Tovar hotel. He spends two days there exploring the area and gets in a lot of walking.

After a couple of days there, he heads west to Kingman, Arizona and decides just to stop and spend the night there and then heads to Vegas the next morning.

With his injured back starting to hurt a little, he thinks a few days in Vegas and a couple of good rub downs, it will be ready for the road again. He will get his bike serviced while he is there.

He finds the local Harley shop and goes in for service and to leave his bike there for protection, not knowing if the hotel would have a secure place to park it. They offered to take him to his hotel, and he had no idea which one he wanted to stay at.

The van driver tells him that the Wynn is a great hotel, and it is right in the middle of the strip. He chooses Wynn.

He gets checked in and heads to his room for his much-needed daily nap. Knowing that the city is up and running twenty-four hours a day, he can sleep in if he wants to and when he gets up, things will be happening.

As he is checking out Fremont Street in the old part of town, he gets a phone call from the Harley place telling him that he is lucky that his bike did not quit on him somewhere between Vegas and New Orleans. The service manager tells him that the intake manifold has a crack in it, and they will have to order the part, and it could take up to five days before they could get it in.

He says to himself, "I don't have enough money with me to stay another five days in Vegas, and where is the bus station," knowing that he was not planning on catching a bus home.

They come and get him and show him the crack, and he says to himself, "Man, I am lucky and I just might buy me a new bike while I am here because I can afford it." With what it is going to cost to get his old bike repaired, that would be a down payment on a new one.

Three hours later, he is in debt big time and ready to get on the road with his brand new bright red Harley. He knows that he will have to find a dealership when he puts five hundred miles on it for a service checkup.

He decides that he should probably head home because there is no telling what Lester has done, and there just might be some new news on the streets. As he was getting ready to leave, not being a family historian, he remembered that his daddy had a brother who lived in Prescott, Arizona and he decided to go there and see if he could possibly find him or some of his kin.

When he gets there, he will get his bike checked over. As he is riding, he says to himself, "Man this thing is nice and yep it costs a lot of money but who cares. I can afford it."

As he is coming into town, he goes right by the Harley shop and pulls in. Everyone comes out to look at his new bike. He is wondering why they are so interested, maybe just because it's new or what.

The first guy says, "Man, we did not know that the new Limited-Edition bike was even for sale." He thinks that the sales guy in Vegas must have seen me coming, and no wonder the damn thing costs so much.

As they are all talking and touching it, he tells them that he wants to get it checked and that he is going to spend the night there, and could they keep it for him. Everyone said, "Yes, we will be glad to."

He checks into a hotel right in the middle of town. This is a really nice-looking town, he says to himself, "And I wonder what there is to do here."

Nap time.

He wakes up around six o'clock and looks in the phone book for Carter's name. He finds two. One is Ms. And the other is William. He says, "My dad always referred to his brother as Bill."

When he dials the number, an elderly sounding man answers the phone and he says, "Is this the William Carter that had a brother that was named Carl?"

There is dead silence and then the man says, "Yes, this is Sand. Who is this?" He tells him that he is Lloyd, Carl's son and that he is in town, and could he possibly visit with him? He told him, "Yes and they plan on meeting tomorrow morning."

He gets on his bike and rides over to what looks like a retirement center. Since he has Bill's unit number, he knocks on the door, and this quite elderly man opens the door and wow, he looked just like his dad.

After a couple of hours talking, he asks Bill if he would like to go and have lunch and he says, "Yes, that would be great since it has been a long time since I even got out of this apartment except to go to the lunch hall with all those old people."

Then it hits him, Bike!

Then he says, "Uncle Bill, are you afraid to ride on the back of a motorcycle?" In a split second he says, "No, I would love to."

They head out to his favorite place, Burger King. After two hours of talking, Uncle Bill says, "Can we just ride around town and see what is going on?" Lloyd tells him, "Let's load up."

Finally, Uncle Bill says that he must go home because he has to pee really bad. After they get that taken care of, Uncle Bill says, "Son, I need to lay down, and can you come by again in the morning?" He says "Yes; he will be glad to."

On the way the next morning, he stops at Burger King and picks up a couple of egg sandwiches and coffee. They talk and enjoy their sandwiches, and then Uncle Bill says, "Son, did you know that you are my only living relative. He continues to say that he had never married and naturally had no children, and I am so glad that you found me, and it makes me know that you are a good person."

Then Uncle Bill says, "Let's walk down to the office for a minute. I want to introduce you to someone and to take care of some business."

He introduces him to a lady by the name of Betty Ford. She is the director of the center, and she looks after him from time to time. They have a short conversation and then Uncle Bill says, "Betty, I have written down some things on this paper and I want you to Notarize it and give my nephew a copy."

She reads it and says, "Bill, are you sure that this is what you want?" He says, "Yep, I wrote it didn't I." Betty says to Lloyd, "This is his last will and testimony, and he is leaving everything to you. Upon his death, he wants to be cremated and when you come to claim what he is leaving you, he wants you to come on your motorcycle and spread his ashes along the road when you go back home."

He does not know what to do or say, and then he gives Uncle Bill a big hug. They spend the rest of the day together and they take another ride together.

The next morning, as he is leaving town, he stops for a minute and says, "I am so lucky to meet my uncle and may God bless him."

He heads home. Five days later, he arrives, tired and with a sore back. Hot shower, bedtime.

The next morning, he checks in with Nancy and Lester. They are both glad that he is back home safe and sound and broke.

The first night he is out, he runs across Pee Wee. They catch up on what has been going on since he has been gone, and he really does not have any news of any kind. They sit and have coffee when they hear what sounds like a gunshot.

Pee Wee says that sounded like it came from Esplanade Ave. They sit and wait to see if there is anything else to go with it. Then they get up and head that way. When they get there, they see nothing and walk all the way to Broad Street. Pee Wee says that it could have been a car backfiring, and Lloyd says that today's cars don't backfire.

They go back to the coffee shop and talk until the fog starts rolling in, and then the sun will try and break through and give them a bright sunny day.

Before he goes to bed, he gives Nancy a call and asks her if she would like to have dinner and hear about his trip. She accepts, and he will meet her at Breaux's at six.

He gets there a little before six, and the owner knows where he likes to sit, and he brings him a glass of water with no ice. She arrives and they have a nice dinner, and when he tells her about meeting his uncle in Prescott and that he really got excited. He said nothing about him being in his will.

As they are walking back to her car, she says, "I have a question for you, and I want the truth." He tells her the only answer she will get from him is the truth.

He is thinking, What is this going to be? I hope it is not some kind of love story or wanting to have kids.

She says, "I would like to know why you have never invited me to stay with you in your apartment?" As he realizes that he had dodged a bullet, he says, "Well, I don't really know and probably one reason is because it is small, and I don't usually keep it too straight. Stuff is laying around, and when Lester used to visit me, there was always another mattress on the floor."

Then he tells her that she is more than welcome to stop by and visit or even stay the night when she wants to because, "You know that I am not there a lot of nights."

As they are leaving the restaurant, he asks her if she would like to spend the night with him in his apartment and she says, "No thanks, I don't have any of my nighttime beauty cream with me." He tells her she can use some of his shaving cream. They laugh and go their separate ways.

He waits for the streetcar to come by, and he will catch the first one that he can. It doesn't matter which way it is going; he always rides them to the turnaround and rides them back to somewhere on Canal Street and gets off. All the operators know him, and they talk during their run.

The first one is headed uptown and all the way around Carrollton and then heads back to Canal Street. On this ride, he sees a couple of people that he knows, and they catch up on where and what he has been doing.

His big story is about his trip and finding his long-lost uncle. As he is going to get off, this one guy that has been riding with them and not being in the conversation says to him, "Can I talk to you a minute, Quarter Man?" He thinks, Where did that name come from? and he thinks, Now what does he have to say that will interest me? But here goes.

The guy says he knows that Spike has made a few trips to Baton Rouge and other dock towns picking up packages and delivering them to people at the dock offices. He asks the guy how he knows that, and why is he telling him this. The guy says that he has been looking for him for about five weeks, and when he saw him, he followed him to Breaux's and waited for him to leave and caught the streetcar one stop before it got to him.

The guy says that his name is Nick and that his girlfriend works in the dock offices, and she told him that she heard a guy say, "Well after his next trip, he will come up missing." She thinks they were talking about Spike. Then he says, "That is all I know, and I knew that you and Spike were friends."

He gives him his phone number and tells him to get in touch with him if he happens to hear anything else, and thanks him and moves away.

Now he says to himself, "I have not seen Spike in a while, and how do I tell him this and then what he should do after he tells him. Oh well, he thinks we can work something out when I see him.

He gives Nick a call and tells him that the next time his wife happens to see Spike, to have him contact him. He says that he will do just that.

Pee Wee sends him a text saying Coffee. He responds by saying ok!

They meet and he says, "You know that shot we heard the other night, well I have this friend of mine that has a habit of hustling other guy's wives, and one took a pop shot at him the other night as he was at the corner of St Peter and Esplanade Ave. and that is the one, we heard."

He tells him that it is none of our business and that he should stay away from the guy, or he just might be the one getting shot. He agrees, and they go their separate ways. He decides to take a walk up Canal Street just to see what is going on in that part of town.

As he is walking back to the Quarter, a car drives by, and someone yells at him and keeps going. Before he knows it, the same car is driving beside him and there are three young punks yelling and shaking their fist at him and he keeps walking.

He watches them and they turn around and start back toward him. Once again, he pays no attention to them until they stop and two of the three jump out and start coming right up to him and just as one of them started to punch or possibly grab him, He pulls out his pistol and says, you are fixing to make a big mistake.

They both fell on the ground trying to stop. The driver drove off and left his two goons lying on the ground looking at him and his gun. They both started saying, please don't shoot us, we were just playing, and we weren't going to do anything.

He tells them both to get on their hands and knees and start crawling towards the end of Canal Street. One hour later with their hands and knees bleeding, he says, ok you can get up now and if I ever see either of you again, the last thing you will ever hear is this pistol going off.

They are still begging for mercy as they are trying to walk away.

He finally gets to his apartment and decides to shut it down for the night now that he had gotten his walk in, and that reminds him, "Has Lester been walking?" Better check with him and see and if he hasn't, he will tell his landlord the General.

The next morning, Nancy calls him and tells him that the chief wants to talk to him for a minute and before she puts the chief on, he asks her if she would like to see his apartment at night and she says, "I will see you at six and now here is the Chief."

When the chief gets on the phone, he is laughing and trying to say, "What in the world were you doing at two o'clock in the morning walking behind two guys that were crawling on their hands and Knees?"

Then he manages to say that while that was going on, a couple of patrolmen on the morning shift saw you and just kept going right on by.

Once he was able to tell the chief what happened, he started laughing all over again and finally just hung up.

He gets a call from Spike and tells him to meet him for coffee when he gets off work. When Spike gets there, he asks him if he had any family in the area, and he tells him no, that he does not and why. He tells him that he is not in a good place where he is working and what he is doing, and you need to quit your job and leave town for your health.

As he is listening to what Lloyd is saying, he does not know what to do but if he is telling me that, it must be true. He tells him, "I really don't have a bunch of relatives that I could go and stay with, and I don't have a lot of money saved up."

Lloyd tells him, "Just wait a minute." He calls his uncle in Prescott. When he answers the phone, he says, "Uncle Bill, this is Lloyd and how are you doing?" They talk for a couple of minutes, and he says, "Uncle Bill I need a favor and you just might be the one person that can help me."

He tells him that he has a friend who needs to get away for a while, and would he mind having a roommate for a while? Uncle Bill asks him if it's a nice-looking lady or some old hard leg. He says, "I am sorry, but it is an old hard leg, and he is really a good kid." He tells him to send him on out and that he will look forward to meeting him.

He gives Spike the address and tells him to go and get his stuff that he really cares about, and to take it with him and we will put your other stuff in storage and meet me at my apartment in twenty minutes.

He meets him at his apartment, and he gives him five hundred dollars and one of his credit cards to be used for gas, and says, "When you get to Prescott, you can mail it back to me." Spike has this weird look on his face, like, "What has just happened to me?"

Lloyd says, "Spike, if you stay around here, you will end up in the river face down."

The next thing you heard was Spike's car cranking up and leaving town.

He gives Nick a call and thanks him, and tells his wife that Spike will not be showing up for work anytime soon and that he owes him a steak dinner. Nick tells him, "You got a deal."

Lester helps him move what little stuff Spike had in his apartment, and then he starts to wonder, "Does he have any relatives and I wonder where and how he ended up here? Guess I will find out someday."

Finally, he and Nancy have a nice dinner, and she stays with him in his apartment. The first thing she says to him when she wakes up is, "How can you sleep with all the clanging and banging going on all night?" He tells her that he hears and sees nothing.

As she is leaving, she tells him that it wasn't so bad that she would be glad to come back. He tells her she is welcome anytime.

Four days later, Spike calls him and tells him that he and Uncle Bill are tight because they both are New York Yankee fans, and he really appreciates him looking out for me. Lloyd tells him that Uncle Bill loves Burger King, and Spike tells him that is where they are going there in about ten minutes.

Lester asks him to drive him across the river in Baton Rouge to pick up some pottery for the General's wife, and he had asked them if it was ok for them to drive their new Lexus. They take their time driving and just talk about everything and nothing.

He is trying hard not to mess up anything in this new high-dollar Lexus. Lester says that he should be sitting in the back and that he could be his chauffeur.

They finally find the place to pick up the pottery and then find a place to grab a bite to eat. They decide to stop at what some people might call a down-and-out pit stop.

As they are having their good hamburgers, two red necks walk up and say, "Hey white boy, don't you have any white friends to have lunch with?" Before another word was spoken, he and Lester had the two guys on the floor putting a whipping on them that they will never forget.

They sit back down at their table and finish their burgers, and about that time two local policemen come in and see the two guys still on the floor and say, "Ok, guys, don't move or do anything foolish or I might have to take you out."

The lead officer asks what happened, and the lady behind the counter said that those two dummies on the floor started it, and those two guys finished it. The guy asked them did they wanted to press charges, and Lester said, "No, I think they have learned their lesson." They leave and laugh all the way back to New Orleans and Lester says, "Look at my hand, I missed the guy with one shot and hit the floor, and it really hurt. More laughter."

He gets up about two fifteen in the morning and decides to check the streets out. Not much is happening at this time. He decides to go to the coffee shop and check things out.

A couple of guys from the vice squad see him and ask if they could sit with him, and he says, "Yes, any time." One of the vice members told him that they arrested a hooker, and she had forty thousand dollars in her purse and two bottles of Cocaine. He continues to say that neither they nor the DEA have seen much of the bad stuff, and this just might be the start.

The other guy says the trouble she is in with the city is nothing what she is going to be in when her people find out she lost their forty thousand dollars and Cocaine. They all agree.

As they are talking, one of the guys gets a call on his radio to come back to the station because the lady that they brought in earlier needs to talk to someone. They say they are on the way and ask Lloyd to go with them.

When they get to the station, the three guys and the lady go into a soundproof room to talk. She starts crying and saying, "With me getting arrested and losing their money and drugs, I will be dead before noon tomorrow." Before the Vice guys could ask him anything, Lloyd says, "Are the people you are having dealings with associated with the docks in any way?"

Both the Vice guys just looked at him and said, "Go ahead." He says, "Does the term Banana seeds ring a bell?" She says, "Yes, that is the code word for Cocaine." Then she says that they brought her in to take care of a guy from Mexico, and then to go back home a few days later.

Then she tells them that she is currently staying in Biloxi, but her home is in Kansas City, where she is a school principal. They ask her does she knows a lot more than she is telling us, and she says, "Yes, a lot more, and she would like to work with the DEA and go into their witness protection program, and I want to get out of this town tonight."

As they are talking to her, she tells them that her cousin works at the dock board, and she has come to New Orleans a few times in the past to take care of some special customer or friend of one of the big boys that has something to do with international shipping.

She goes on to say that when she flew in, a guy by the name of Spike would always pick her up at the airport and bring her into town, where a room would be waiting for her.

Then she drops a bomb on them. She says that the word on the street is that "if you are nice and have a few extra bucks, you can get out of town without being charged if you are caught with any sizeable number of drugs."

The lead vice guy gives her his business card, and they hide it inside the lining of her purse and tell her that if anything like what she has said goes down, to let him know and to please be careful.

They call the local DEA chief and wake him up, and ask her to come down to their office and not to wait until later in the morning.

When he gets there, he tells them that this better be good, or he will have their hides, and who is this ragtag standing here? Talking about Lloyd. One of the vice guys says that he is a deaf mute and just likes to hang around the police station.

He leaves and heads back to finish his coffee, and wonders what the DEA chief will end up doing. His past dealings have not been what the big boys at DEA headquarters want to see.

As he is heading back to his apartment, wondering how an educated person like the girl they just arrested could get involved in the hooker and drug business. Guess they just don't get paid enough.

Before he gets there, the vice guys drive up and ask him to get in their car and say, "Let's go to breakfast." They head out to their favorite hangout and order breakfast.

As they are eating, one of the guys asks him, "How in the world did you know about the banana seeds?" He tells them about going to Baton Rouge with a clerk from the dock company and picking up a package from a ship from Honduras, which was labeled banana seeds.

Then he tells them that a guy caught up with him one night and gave him some info about something that might be going down at the dock company, and before it could happen, he helped the guy get out of town. Then the guy says, "ok, tell us about you and the guys crawling down Canal Street on their hands and knees."

As he was telling his story, they all were laughing so loud that their server came over and asked them to try and be a little quitter. They try.

He finally gets to bed, and before he thinks, "Why am I doing this? I just can't keep staying up all night and getting involved in bad things. I just might have to move to Prescott and stay with Uncle Bill until he gets out of here."

As he is sleeping, there is a knock on his door, and it is Pee Wee saying, "Hey man, open up, I have some news for you." He gets up and opens his door, and he is so excited that he can hardly talk. He tells him to turn his T V on and watch the news.

He does and all local stations are running a story about a federal sting operation in which the local chief of the DEA has been arrested for trying to make a drug deal with an undercover federal agent.

Just about that time, both vice guys hit his door, going crazy. Pee Wee doesn't have any idea what is happening with all the high fives and hugging. He manages to get into a corner and just watches.

The vice guys say, "Hey, let's go and get something to eat, and you can come with us." As they are eating, the vice guy's phone rings, and it is the undercover agent asking where he is and when he tells her, she says that she will meet them there.

When she arrives, Lloyd says, "You are the coolest hooker I have ever known, and while living here, I have known a few as friends, so don't get any ideas."

After their nearly two-hour meeting and coffee fill, she says to the vice guys, "I am being serious when I say this that you two guys are two of the most professional people that I have worked with, and if either or both of you want a job as a DEA agent, you have it." Then she says, "Sorry Lloyd, we can't use a mute. More laughter."

They offer to drive him back to his apartment, and he says, "No thanks, Pee Wee and I will walk back." He says, "Hey, why me?" and he tells him that he looks bad, and he needs some exercise.

Chapter 5
Big time arrest

Later in the afternoon, the T V stations broke for another news release saying that five people who worked at the dock board offices have been arrested and were all involved with the former DEA chief here in town.

He says to himself, "Man, I am glad Spike is out of town and I bet they will want him as a witness in the future when everything goes to trial. Maybe he just can't be located when that time comes, and I may even be missing also."

A couple of days later as he is checking his mail, he gets an announcement about a class reunion that is being planned. He thinks, "Now do I want to go to that thing and see all those fat classmates? Well maybe," he says to himself and guesses it will be a nice get together.

He sends in his confirmation and money and decides just to wear some of his Key West clothes. Everyone might think I am well-traveled, but I have been to Vegas. That is something for a country boy from East Texas.

The city is still buzzing about all the DEA stuff, and it has even been on the national news. That is something that they really don't want everyone to know, but it is way too late.

He thinks, if we can overcome these hurricanes, we can overcome this, and it just might keep other drug people out of here. "We have a great city," he says to himself.

As he is heading to his class reunion, he starts thinking about all the things he did growing up in a small town and only about thirty-five seniors; he is wondering how many have died and how many married their high school sweethearts and are now divorced.

Then it hits him that Betty Brown, the love of his life. He wonders if she will be there and thinks that, since she was so smart, she really made it big time.

When he gets to his hometown, he decides just to ride around and see what has changed and see just how much it has changed. When he sees the changes, it makes him feel a little sad to see all the old buildings torn down and replaced with new and modern ones.

He checks into his room, showers, takes an hour nap and gets dressed in his Key West clothes and heads out to the reunion.

As he walks in the room, everyone claps and yells, "Welcome home Lloyd". He did not know what to do or say. They all come to meet him and hug and shake hands.

As they are getting ready to eat, big Al stands up and brings everyone up to date on the ones that have gone on before us and where the ones that could not make it. He was wondering where Betty was.

As they are eating and talking, in walks Dr. Betty Brown dressed in her scrubs. When she sees him, she makes a beeline and grabs him and says, "I was praying that you would be here, and I still love you."

Everyone cheers and says, "Well, he came all the way on his motorcycle just to hear you say that." He does not know what to say, and he finally manages to say, "I was hoping you would feel and say that because you are still the one for me." Once again, cheers.

As the gathering is closing, they make plans to see one another tomorrow at the luncheon and see what happens from there.

When he gets back to his room, he is still awake at three in the morning thinking about Betty and being the night person he is, he thinks it is normal to be still awake.

He is up and dressed in his boots and jeans, and a somewhat wrinkled shirt and heads out to the luncheon. Everyone is having a good time. He and Betty sit together. They are not concerned about what is going on around them.

As the reunion is breaking up, Big Al says that with all of our classmates dying off, maybe we should have another one next year at the same time and place. Everyone agrees.

Betty invites him over to her house to catch up on how he has been doing, and that she had heard that he was hurt while working and that he had broken his back.

He tells her that it is true and that he was unable to walk for a time, and then on a walker and then a cane, and finally he could walk ok. She says, "Riding that bike is not the best thing for you to be doing because I am a back surgeon."

She then tells him that she had been married for a few years and that it never worked out, and she had been single for a number of years and a lot of times, she would wonder if you were married and had kids.

He looks in her eyes and says, "I never got over losing you and have had a few girlfriends, but nothing really serious on my part." She says, "I know how you feel, and maybe now that we know where both of us are, do you think that maybe someday we just might be able to grow old together."

He tears up and says, "I would love that." Then he wonders to himself, "Can I settle down and live a normal life, and me not being able to work and her being a doctor, that just might not work?"

They have dinner and talk very late, and he goes back to his room and decides to load up and go back to the city. He calls her and tells her that he is going to go back tonight, and he will call her tomorrow. She tells him that she knew that he would.

It is a tough ride back. Thinking about what he will do, and whether he could become a good husband? The thought scares him. As he rides into the city at four in the morning, he feels relief and puts his bike up and checks out the streets.

As he is walking to his apartment, he says to himself, "Maybe it was a mistake to go to the reunion, but it's too late for that. Now what to do?" he thinks.

He decides to get some coffee before he gets to his apartment and sees who's out and about tonight. He sees Rusty, an old, retired army guy who has taken up residence in the city and always has a good story to tell about his thirty years in the army.

His son is a popular attorney here in the city and keeps tabs on him. He is eighty years old and seems to be in great shape, and he says, "I walk five miles a day." During the summer months, you will see him out at night, and when it turns cold, his son ships him to a relative somewhere below Tampa.

He thinks to himself, "Why do I stay here when it gets cold and my back really hurts? Maybe I should do the same thing. I wonder what the weather is like in Prescott in the winter." He checks, and it's way too cold for him and his bad back because he knows that as he gets older, his back will be a real problem.

As he decides to go to bed, as he is laying in his bed, he thinks about Betty and where that might end up, but with reservations?

Lester calls him and says that they need to make another trip to the other side of Baton Rouge and pick up some more pottery for the general's wife, and they are not going to stop at the same place as before.

On the way, Lloyd asks Lester did he knows anyone in Florida who could give him some info about when and where to visit in the winter months. He tells him that he has an uncle who lives in Naples, and it is really a nice place and expensive during the winter months.

They stop and have lunch, and Lester says, "ok, what's bugging you and why are you wondering about a place in the winter?" He tells him about the reunion, the cold months affecting his back, and maybe just starting over.

Lester says, "You know something, the only relatives that are still alive that I know of is my uncle in Naples. Maybe I should start thinking about somewhere in the winter months, but I am really enjoying being with the general and his wife."

Lloyd says, "What about you and Miss Taylor at the V.A. office?" He laughs and says, "After two dinner dates, I smelled a skunk in the wood pile and checked it out on that. Nice, but since I am going to get some back pay and I don't know how much or when, but if I do get a nice lump sum, maybe we both should move to Key West and open up a pie or cookie store, and I would probably be one of the few black people there."

For some reason, he is not happy anymore and seems to be depressed, whatever that is. He likes traveling even though it makes his back hurt, but the new bike is a lot more comfortable than the one that died in Vegas.

There is a funeral procession headed into the Quarter, and he decides to go and watch. He sees a lot of people that he knows waving their umbrellas and doing the slow shuffle. Dragging up the rear of the group is Lester. He motions for him to join in the parade, and he decides to.

They go to the cemetery, and then when they head back into the quarter, everyone is dancing and singing to the beat of the band. And as they are starting to break up and go their separate ways, Lester gives him a piece of paper that looks like a bank statement.

He opens it up and cannot believe the balance that was in his account. The government had reimbursed him for a lot of years since he had not received his disability. It was mega dollars and way more than it would take to open a pie or cookie store in Key West.

They have just celebrated their second anniversary of L & L's cookie and pie store in Key West, Florida. While they like the area, the Crescent City keeps calling them back. After a lot of discussion, they decided to sell the business and move back.

Once a buyer was found, they loaded up and headed back. With money in their pockets, they decided to take their time to go and do a little sightseeing.

Somehow, they ended up in Charlotte, North Carolina, at a professional football game. As the game is over and they are headed to their bikes, Lester says, "Now didn't we leave the Keys headed to New Orleans, and what are we doing here in Charlotte?"

Three days later, they arrive in New Orleans, tired and looking for a place to lay their heads. Lester calls the general and finds out that his wife has passed away and that his garage apartment was just like it was when he left it, and to come on by and get the key.

They both bunk in for a while, and then Lloyd calls Nancy, and she is elated to hear that he is back in town. She was sure that the chief would also be because there had been some things going on in the city that no one could get a handle on, and on a number of occasions, he would say, "Man, I wish Lloyd was still here."

Then he gets in touch with Tommy, and he says, "Man, you are here just in time to give me a hand with something that has been going on in and around the docks."

Being gone for a couple of years, there will be a lot of people there who won't know him.

He is back in his old apartment, and he and Nancy are planning on having dinner together. She tries to bring him up to date on who and what has been happening in the city since he has been gone. He finds out that a lot of his old friends have died naturally, been shot, killed or just vanished off the face of the earth.

Tommy tells him that the passport thing has started up again after going dark for a couple of years, and he would like him to try and see how and where that is getting done.

Lester has decided to go and visit relatives in Texas, Missouri, Tennessee, and Ohio and does not know when he will be back, but he will keep in touch.

After lunch with Nancy, he gets with the chief and asks him did he had any idea about any wrongdoing going on in and around the dock area. He tells him that he does not, and if he hears anything, he will let him know.

For some reason, he does not believe him and that bothers him. He is hoping that he is not involved with anything, and he should not have talked to him about anything.

Knowing that the dock area is always hiring, he gets cleaned up and goes to their personnel office and fills out an application. He shows that he has just moved there from Key West and lists a number of fake jobs, and when he needs a reference, he puts down Lester's name and number and then calls him, and they get their stories straight.

Fortunately, he had kept his driver's license current. He could always buy a car and Uber or do inner city deliveries. Two days later, he gets a call from one of the companies that has offices right in the middle of the docks and offices in Baton Rouge and Mobile.

When he follows up on the phone calls, they tell him that they have a couple of openings, and which one would he like? He could be a dock worker, do house cleaning on incoming ships, learn to operate a crane or be a courier. He takes the courier position.

He has to take a drug test, but that would make no difference. He passes, and they tell him to report the next day at eight o'clock and be ready to drive to Mobile and deliver some manifest papers and come right back. He is thinking that he might just stop and check out a casino on the way back.

As soon as he walks into his new place of employment, a lady gives him an envelope and shows him the address in Mobile, and to have fun and not stop in Biloxi at the casinos. He laughs and says, "Never and I guess I will see you tomorrow."

On the way, he calls Daniel to check and see what the DEA are up to. He gets him and they meet, and he rides to Mobile with him. He gets caught up on everything that has been going on over the last two years.

As they are having dinner at one of the casinos, Daniel asks him how well he knows the chief of police in New Orleans. He breaks into a sweat and finally manages to say, I know him probably better than anyone else outside of his family.

Daniel proceeds to tell him that he knew of some major drug dealings in McComb, and when they ran the plates on all of the cars at this meeting, the car came back registered to the chief, and does he have any kids that might have used his car?

He tells him that he does not have any kids and is single. Daniel then tells him that one of the cars was listed on the dock board where you are now employed, and he just might have to take him to jail. Lloyd says, "You might have a problem because my gun is bigger than yours, and I have my hand on it right now."

Before he leaves, Daniel gives him all the information on the car that was registered to the dock company and the person who was driving it. He thinks to himself, "That sounds like the lady that I met in the coffee room when they were interviewing me. Lester, where are you when I need you?"

He gets home late but calls Tommy and brings him up to date on what he had heard for the day, and that as soon as Lester gets back, he needs to put him on his payroll, or maybe he can get him a job with him.

The next morning, he calls Lester and wakes him up. He is in Memphis, headed home. After they talk, he tells Lloyd that he will be there in a couple of days, and they will talk then.

He still does not like working in the daytime, and he misses the streets at night. He thinks that he will check the streets out at night over the weekends. That is when most of the stuff is going on anyway.

Friday night and an LSU ballgame, Saturday and a professional game in the Superdome, Sunday, things are starting to happen. The ladies of the night do not know him, so when he goes to one of the nightclubs, they start hitting on him.

Once they see that they are wasting their time, they move on, and actually some of them are nice looking. He talks to one, and she is a schoolteacher from Jackson, Mississippi, and when there is a big weekend in the city, she drives down to make a little extra spending money, and she says, "It's tax-free."

He then tells her that if he was a really bad person, he would have the boys in blue come and get her and take her downtown, but he will just finish his coke and move on. She thanked him.

When he gets into his new office area, he goes into the coffee room and gets one of the fresh donuts and starts looking at the local paper. He is there for two hours before anyone else comes in and speaks to him.

The guy's name is Rusty, and he is the president of the dock board. "What is your name?" he asks. He tells him that his name is Lloyd and that today is his second day working here, and they had sent him to Mobile on Friday and that he was really thankful to have a good job.

Rusty says, "What I like to hear, a happy employee and if you stick around, you just might be president of the dock board someday."

After his third donut, and as he is getting ready to leave and just go somewhere, the coffee lady comes in and asks him who had been eating all of the donuts, and he tells her he had one and that Rusty had been in there with him.

She tells him that her name is Sally Strong. She has been working there for fifteen years, and when she is not cleaning, they have her running all over the country delivering flowers and packages to different people. "One time, I had to go all the way to Laredo, Texas, and that trip took a whole week. I brought back a big package of banana seeds, and I think they are going to start raising bananas in Mississippi." He nearly falls out of his chair.

He gets in touch with Daniel and tells him that the car that they saw in McComb was the person from the dock company, and she had told him that they sent her to Laredo, Texas, to pick up a box of banana seeds.

The lady who interviewed him finds him and tells him that if he wanted to just wait at home, he could go on and if and when they needed him, she would call him. He is out the door.

Lester finally gets into town, and they go and get something to eat. He tells him about Sally Strong being a nice-looking African American lady and the way she talked; she was single. They make plans to meet after dark and check out the streets.

While taking his nap, he gets a call from Spike, and the first thing he says is, "Hey, do you know where Uncle and I are?" He says, "In a Burger King somewhere," and Spike tells him that they are in Phoenix and going to take in a baseball game. Once he finds out that both of them have a new girlfriend, he gets off the phone.

They meet at nine o'clock and start walking the entire Quarter, all along the river and into the vacant warehouse areas. He checks out where Dolly had been living, and there were a couple of guys in there, and they ask them for some Georges, and they give them a couple and are on their way to St. Charles Avenue.

They catch the streetcar and ride it to the end, and then ride it back. Nothing seems to be going on, and just as they get off, they hear three- or four-gun shots and people yelling and they have no idea where they had come from. They both stop and listen.

Just then, they hear a car in a hurry heading their way with loud exhaust and just as it passes them, they see a flash and then the sound of a gunshot and they both hit the sidewalk. He takes out his gun and just hopes that they will come back by.

They go to where all of the yelling is, and there on the sidewalk are two guys and their girlfriends or wives, he is guessing are going crazy. Lester tries to calm them down, and Lloyd has called nine-one-one.

When he checks the two down guys, one is dead, and the other one is not doing too well. Once the police get there, they all know him and he and Lester just back away and let them do their jobs.

Lester asks him, "Now I wonder why two couples are in this part of downtown at this time of night." Nothing is open and they or six blocks from Canal Street and the start of the Quarter.

Two hours later, the police finally got the dead guy wrapped up and hauled away, and the other guy was long gone to the hospital. Then the police start asking them one question after another. One of the guys did not know Lloyd, and he was trying to be the tough guy and was not getting anywhere and then a lieutenant walks up and says, "Hey, where in the world have you two guys been for the last few years?"

Lester says, "Making pies and sandwiches in Key West."

They all end up at the French Quarter coffee shop and were still talking after the sun breaks thru the early morning fog. The new policeman could not keep up with everything that was going on.

Since it was morning, Lloyd tells Lester to come and go with him, and he just might find him a job or maybe a new girlfriend. He tells him, "No job and a new girlfriend, maybe."

As they are having coffee, Sally comes doing her thing and says, "Don't you two guys eat all the donuts." When she sees Lester, she says, "Hey, aren't you that homeless guy who solved the murder of the hairdresser and his girlfriend?'

He did not know what to say, and Lloyd said, "Yes, he is, and he got all of that reward money, and he does not have a girlfriend." She says, "Honey, you can have as many donuts as you want, and my name is Sally Summers."

As they are talking, a guy comes in that he had never seen and tells Lloyd that this packet needs to be taken to Baton Rouge and exchange it for another one and let me know when you get back. My name is Junior.

They go to Baton Rouge, and Lester sleeps all the way. They find where they are to go, exchange packages and head back to town. Lester is still asleep.

He takes him home, goes to the office and gives Junior his package and goes home. He gives Nancy a call and tells her he will see her tomorrow, and good night.

The next morning, as he is walking towards the docks, he hears the familiar sound of the car that possibly shot the two guys and then took a potshot at him and Lester. When it passes him, he notices that there is a female driving, and she is by herself. Before he knew it, she had turned down a side street and was out of sight, and he did not get the plate number, but he would be in that exact spot at the same time tomorrow morning.

He hangs around the offices until noon and then leaves and goes back to his apartment. Lester calls and tells him that he is taking Sally out to dinner, and asks if he and Nancy want to join them. He tells him to let him check and he will call him back, and then he thinks to himself, how is he going to take her to dinner, not on his bike, he hoped.

He calls him back and asks him how he was going to take her to dinner and not on his bike. He asks, and Lester says, "The general had given me his wife's old Mercury, and I am now a car owner, and I have to get it transferred into my name."

Everything is set, Lester and Salley and Lloyd and Nancy in the back seat, and they are going across the lake to have a seafood dinner.

As they are leaving the restaurant, the police pull in behind them and start flashing their lights and activating their siren. Lloyd says, "I hope your license is current and up to date."

The officer comes to his window and asks him for his license, insurance and registration. He digs in the glove box and finds an insurance card and then the registration, and gives it to the officer. He takes the info and walks back to his car and after a few minutes, he tells Lester to please get out of the car and he does as he is asked and when the office tells him to turn around and to put his hands behind his back, he asks him why and what he had done.

He then tells him, "Do what I say, or I am going to tase you." When Lloyd heard that, he put his window down and showed the policeman his New Orleans Police ID. The guy did not know what to do, and Lloyd asked, "Can I get out of the car?" The officer said, "Yes."

The office said that he saw that the inspection sticker on the car was out of date, and then he saw Lester driving a car that is registered to someone on St. Charles Ave. He thought something did not look quite right and decided to do a traffic stop and check everything out.

Then Lester had heard all he wanted to, and he says, "No, you see a black guy driving a car that is registered to someone who lives on St. Charles Ave., and you were thinking that you just might have recovered a stolen Mercury. And if I did not do what you said, then you could tase me, right?"

The office starts to try and say the right thing, and before Lester could say anything else, Lloyd tells him just shut up and tell the man to have a nice rest of the night, and we will get our asses across the lake and in bed.

After all was said and done, the policeman apologized and told them to have a safe trip home. Needless to say, that ruined their night, and as they were dropping Sally off at her house, Lloyd said, "Sally, I would appreciate it if you would never say anything about me having a police officer ID." She said, "What ID?"

They get back to town, and Lloyd and Nancy get out into the Quarter, and Lester and Sally head to who knows where.

The next morning, when he gets to his new job really excited about doing nothing. Junior comes and gives him an envelope and says, "Here is your paycheck." He opens it, and it's just cash. All hundred-dollar bills. He thinks this is nice because, "I may not have to pay taxes on it."

Nancy calls him and says that the chief would like to see him when he gets a chance to stop by. He checks with Junior and asks him if they have anything for him to do in the next few minutes, then he has a doctor's appointment, and he should be back pretty quick.

The chief asked him, "Do you know a lot of people at the Bureau?" He had a little hot flash and said, "My friend from years ago retired and moved to Arizona. Why are you asking?"

He tells him that you know they think they can tell everyone in law enforcement what they can and cannot do. Lloyd says that may have been true years ago, but that is not the case today. Then the chief says, "What about the DEA? There is another little sweat."

Lloyd tells him that he thinks that the DEA is more concerned with the big-time boys rather than some local guy doing a little drug business. Whatever he had told him, he seemed ok with it.

As he leaves, he is thinking, this guy is my friend and would do anything for me that he asked, and now here he is messing around with some type of drug thing.

As he is walking back to his job, he gets a call from Mattie, and it scares him because with her son at St. Jude in Memphis, he automatically thinks the worst. When he answers, she is crying and then he starts crying. She finally manages to tell him that her little boy is cancer-free and has been discharged from St. Jude, and she and her husband are happy, and everything is just great. He hung up thirty minutes later.

He and Lester are sitting in the Quarter coffee shop when they look at one another and Lester says, "There is that sound we heard right after the shooting the other night." Lester gets up and walks right in front of the car, and they have to stop before hitting him. The driver yells, "Hey old man, watch where you are walking." He says, "Oh, I am sorry, I thought you were a real person driving that sharp-looking Mercery.

As he is doing that, Lloyd is writing down the plate number. Just as he gets out of the way, the driver says, "Hey, you don't want me to get out of this car and take care of you, do you?" Lester says, Hey boy, don't let anything but fear and God hold you back, so come on."

Lloyd had already taken his gun out of its holster just in case something started to go bad. Lester moves completely out of the way, and the guy drives off.

They get in touch with Nancy and give her the plate number. She calls them back and says that the plate is registered to a two thousand eighteen Volvo. The car was a fairly new Mercury that was seen leaving the shooting area, and they will never forget the sound that it made.

While at the shooting and trying to help out, before he left the area, he picked up an empty casing from a forty-caliber pistol. With the guy roaming the streets, he decides to go and talk to the chief and then a detective that he knows, and they can put out a BOLO (Be on the lookout) for the car and to be very careful because they are armed and dangerous.

Nancy calls and asks him to meet her at Canal and St. Charles in thirty minutes. He does, and she gives him a portable radio that he can listen to and communicate with the police department. His call number is seven seven four.

After breakfast at Mother's, he heads to his cash-paying job at the docks. Sally greets him and tells him that Lester is a really nice guy and that he treats her like a real lady. He thinks to himself, "Oh me, here we go."

Later in the morning, Junior comes in and tells him that he needs to make another trip to Mobile and pick up a box from the same place that he had delivered the other package to and be careful because it could weigh as much as a hundred pounds.

He tells Junior that he might stop off at a casino on the way back, and if he does, he will see him in the morning. He says, "Ok, but be sure and lock your car because that package is very valuable."

Calls Lester and asks him to ride with him, and they are on their way. They talk about this and that and decide to go to Prescott, Arizona to visit Spike and Uncle Bill.

They pick up the package and give Daniel a call to find out where he is, and maybe they can meet up. He can't because he is in Jackson in federal court, where some of the earlier people involved with the transportation thing that went down.

At the casino, they grab a bite to eat and decide to play the twenty-five-cent slots and just waste their money. That gets boring in a hurry, and Lester moves into the poker room and starts playing Texas Hold' Um. He starts with six hundred dollars. Three of his and three of Lloyd's.

They had agreed to leave in three hours, no matter how he was doing at the poker table. While Lester is doing that, he is hanging out in the pool room playing by himself. Before he knows it, Lester is saying, "Ok, it's time to go. I have my twenty dollars, and here is your twenty."

On the way back, they get serious about going to Arizona to see Spike and Uncle Bill. Lester has never seen that part of the country and is looking for to the trip.

He delivers the heavy package to Junior and then tells him that his uncle in Arizona is really sick and that he may need to take off a few days and go and see him, and since he does not have a car, he will be using his bike and which takes a lot more time.

He tells him that he has to make a quick trip to Baton Rouge in the morning, and then he can go on his trip. He checks with Daniel to see if there is a DEA agent in New Orleans that he can trust and start working with. He tells him that he will get back with him later.

Nancy gives him a call and asks if they could have dinner because she wants to talk with him in private. They agree to meet at Rico's at seven because they always put him in the very back at a table in the corner.

They meet, and she tells him that she is concerned about what is going on with the chief and some of the people he sees. He closes his door and talks really low, and she also saw a deposit slip on his desk for twenty thousand dollars, and he does not make that kind of money being chief of police.

He then tells her that she is right, and that the DEA has been watching him because his personal car was seen at a drug house in McComb here a while back, and he hates it because he likes him, and they're friends. But if he is covering up for drug people because of his position, shame on him.

Daniel calls him and tells him that there is an agent who was born and raised in the city and has been wanting to get transferred back there, and he has applied for a transfer and should be calling him sometime today.

He goes and gets his bike out of storage and has it serviced. While at the bike shop, he sees them servicing a brand-new top-of-the-line bike. He talks to the guy working on it, and he tells him that it is the newest one made by Harley, and they got it in yesterday and an African American came in and saw it and paid cash for it because he is going to take a road trip out west. He tells the service guy, "You've got to be kidding." He says, "Nope, that is the truth."

He calls Lester and tells him that he can't go on their trip because he has fallen and hurt his back. He could hear the disappointment over the phone. Lester says, "Oh, is there anything I can do to help him?" and Lloyd says, "Yes, there is." He asks him to go to the bike shop and take it to his apartment, and when he feels better, they can go on their trip. Then he tells him that when he was at the shop, he saw the service people working on a brand new bike and the guy said that they had just gotten it in and they found a crack in the manifold and a guy had bought it and they don't have the new parts and it could take up to eight weeks before that can fix it.

Finally, Lloyd says, "Hello, is there anyone there?" Lester finally says, "You know, you are my very best friend and actually my only friend, but you are a lying SOB and they crack up laughing." With that behind them, he starts getting his stuff together.

Later in the day, he gets a call from a guy who says that his name is Tucker and that he is a friend of Daniel and that his transfer request has been approved, and he can't move for at least four or five weeks. That is good, he tells him because he is leaving to go out of town, and he could be gone that long.

The next morning, he makes his trip to Baton Rouge and picks up a totally different looking package, and it does not have banana seeds on it. He thinks, "Oh well, I can't worry about it." He delivers it to Junior and tells him that he will be leaving tomorrow, and he will see him when he gets back. Junior tells him he hopes his uncle gets better.

They plan on riding at night, and Lester has to have his bike serviced after the first five hundred miles. The first morning, they are in San Antonio getting his bike serviced. Everyone had to check it out because it was the newest and best of the best.

Since neither one of them had ever been there, they decided to spend the day looking around. They check out the Alamo and the Riverwalk. Since they had been up all night, after they got his bike, they checked into a room and slept until nine that night and then got back on the road.

They end up in El Paso ready to get into bed. They sleep until around six and are up and showered and have eaten, and are ready to get back on the road. They take a northern route and finally end up in Santa Fe. They check out the moon crater and finally end up in Flagstaff, and then up to the Grand Canyon. They were able to get a room at the famous hotel on the south rim, and they decided to spend a couple of days there doing nothing.

As they are leaving there, Lloyd asks Lester if he wants to go to Vegas, and he tells him No thanks. They end up in Sedona for a couple of days and then on to Prescott. Spike and Uncle Bill are glad to see them, and the reunion is on.

After a week there, they are getting a little bored and start talking about getting back on the road. Lester tells him that he has not noticed a pie and sandwich shop in Prescott, and what did he think? Later, he replies and looks at him like he is nuts.

Spike has found a home, they are glad for him, and it has given Uncle Bill someone to go to Burger King with, and he has pep in his step.

They get their bikes serviced and once again, everyone is interested in Lester's bike, and he loves it. They leave and take six days to get back home. As they are eating one day, Lester says that maybe we should take a trip up to New York and he says, "You must be crazy and if I take another trip like this, it will be to Key West, and Lester says, "Ok, when are we going?"

Once home, he takes a couple of days to get rested up, and then he lets Junior know that he is back. With no trip in the works, he sleeps all day and is out walking the streets at night. He sees a lot of his old friends and hears gossip.

While they were gone, there was a shooting on Broad Street and a guy was killed and at the scene, they recovered a forty caliber casing. When he hears this, he gets with the detectives, and they compare it to the one that he had picked up earlier, and they matched. So, now they know that they have the same shooter.

Tucker, the new DEA agent, gives him a call and they meet for lunch. They meet at Rico's and talk for a couple of hours. He finds out that Daniel, the agent that he hooked up with in Biloxi, is one of the top agents in the DEA and will probably one day be the chief of the department.

Tucker tells him, "We know someone has a system that is working, and that someone is moving a lot of drugs through New Orleans. It finally manages to hit the streets of New York, and I just hope I might become a pain in their butts so they move somewhere else."

Spike calls him and tells him, "Uncle Bill died in his sleep. A while back, we went to a lawyer's office, and he fixed his will so that if anything happened to him, his little house, car, and money in the bank would go to me. He didn't have any children, so that won't be a problem. I guess I'll just stay here until I die, and I'll leave everything to you. Thanks for getting me out of here."

He and Lester are having breakfast before he goes to bed, and they hear the familiar sound of the car they think was involved in the shooting, the one that called Lester an old man. As it drives by, he takes down the tag number and says, "I'll give it to Nancy later to check out." The last one was registered to a Volvo, and the guy is driving a Mercury.

They both say that they need to come up with some way to get this guy off the streets, and he tells Lester to go and walk in front of him again and see if he will run over you. He says that is not going to happen.

He gives Nancy the tag number, and it comes back registered to a Toyota SUV in Gonzales. When he hears that, he asks her to check with the chief and ask him if he had a few minutes to visit after lunch. She checks and she tells him to come on at any time.

In their meeting, he asks him had he has done anything about a BOLO for that Mercury with the funny sound yet? He tells him no, that he had forgotten to because he has been busy doing other stuff. While in his office, the chief gets on his radio and asks the captain in charge of traffic to come to his office.

He does, and Lloyd brings him up to date on the shooting that happened about two months ago and that he had picked up a forty-caliber shell casing at the scene, and then he found out that they had recovered another forty-caliber casing at the Broad Street shooting. Then he tells him that he had checked out the car's plates and they have come back registered to a Volvo, and the car is a mercury.

The Captain asks the chief what he wanted him to do, and he finally says, "I guess you better get a BOLO out and pick the guy up, and then we can go from there." As he and the Captain are leaving, he whispers, "Here is my card, call me.'

He calls him and they agree to meet at Rico's in an hour. They meet, and he tells Lloyd that everyone is talking about the chief not doing his job and always seems to have other things on his mind. Lloyd says, "Maybe it's time for him to retire and ride off into the sunset."

Lloyd tells the captain to put out the BOLO and to be careful, and that he is going back and talk with the chief. He just walks into his office and closes the door when their radios start going off. The police had stopped the Mercury, and the driver had tried to shoot the policeman who went up to the driver's window, and he had returned fire, hitting the driver.

Everything was going on. An awful lot of radio stations are saying this and that, as expected. They find out that the driver was shot, and he was a convicted felon on parole and had three different guns in his car.

Once all of the excitement settles down, Lloyd tells the chief that he needs to take some time off because he is tired and not doing the job that he is capable of and that he was sure that he had some comp time built up and he would still be paid.

After talking for three hours, the chief agreed to take some time off and that he was going to visit some relatives in Mississippi. Lloyd thinks, "Here we go again."

On the evening news, the stations are announcing that the chief has decided to take some personal time off just to rest and recharge his batteries and that the captain of the traffic division will be acting chief until further notice. Then they covered the traffic stop that turned into a shootout, with the driver being shot and not killed.

Now what bothers him is the chief saying that he has relatives in Mississippi, and the DEA was watching the place he was visiting earlier, and where did he get the twenty thousand dollars from that Nancy saw the deposit slip on his desk.

When he and Tucker meet again, he asks him if he thought it would be a good idea for him to take his old job at the docks, and maybe he could figure out what was going on, and he thought it would be a great idea and they are off to meet with Junior.

They tell him that Tucker is his cousin and that he has just moved back home and needs a steady job for a while until he gets settled. He thinks that is a good idea, and he can start tomorrow.

He is so glad that he is out of that mess, and now maybe he can do his regular job checking out the streets at night.

As he is sitting on a bench in Jackson Square, his phone rings, and it's the police chief wanting to meet with him. He tells him to come to the Quarter coffee shop, and he will meet him there. As he is waiting, he sees this new fancy bright red pickup pull into a handicap parking place and out comes the chief.

An hour later, he is in his new truck and heads to Mississippi. He told Lloyd that he had been saving his money and finally had enough to buy himself a new sixty-thousand-dollar truck cash.

He gets in touch with Daniel and tells him to let him know if he sees a new bright red Dodge pickup at the Mississippi house because the chief had just bought one.

Around midnight, he gets a call from Daniel, and he tells him that he is at the casino and there is a new bright red Dodge truck parked in a handicap spot and could it possibly be the chiefs? He tells Daniel that it probably is and that he made a side trip before heading up to McComb to visit relatives.

He says to himself again that he hates to see the chief get involved in something that could put him away for the rest of his life and maybe one day, he just might get the guts to sit him down and tell him what is going on.

Tucker gives him a call and wakes him up at three in the afternoon. Once he knows that he is a night owl, he will not be bothering him during the day, but could he meet him somewhere later tonight? They have agreed to meet at the City Kitchen at eight.

They meet, and he tells Lloyd that Junior came in and gave him his first week's pay in cash. He tells him that was the way that they had been paying them, and the nice thing is that you don't have to claim it on your taxes. He then tells him that he has to make a delivery to Lafayette tomorrow and meet a guy at the EXXON station across from the Interstate at noon and to swap packages.

Lloyd says that one is drugs, and the other is cash, probably, and to try and get the plate number off of the vehicle that the people you are meeting, if possible. Man, this is complicated Tucker says. "It will only get better," Lloyd says, "And a lot more interesting."

They go their separate ways, and he starts his nightly stroll around the city. He sees Lester and Dolly having coffee at the coffee shop. He joins them and finds out that she has quit working at the dock business because too many funny things are going on. Like what he asks?

She tells him that all different kinds of people are in and out, always exchanging packages and one guy even left his Passport on the table and he was from some country that I could not even read the writing.

Then she says, "When I took it into the office, you would have thought I had found a winning lottery ticket." They grabbed it and took off into the big boss's office.

She then says that when she was cleaning the big boss's office, there was a box under his desk, and when she moved it to get to the trash can, she noticed that it was full of cash. She pushed it back and left the trash there.

Lester tells her that her quitting was the best thing that she could do, and they were talking about taking a trip together and were wondering if you and Nancy might want to go?

Sounds good, he says, "I will check with her tomorrow, but with the new acting chief, she may not be able to get time off, and where would we be going on the trip?"

He says, "Key West or Washington D D.C.?" Then Lloyd says that there is no way that he is going to Washington, D.C. with all those crazy people there, and you don't need to see the Wall of Honor because all of your friends' names are on it.

They leave, and he checks out all of the empty warehouses along the tracks and then moves over to St. Charles Avenue and ends up at Lee Circle, sitting on a bench. Then he hears footsteps. He takes his gun out and listens. They stop for a minute, and then he hears them again and then he hears someone say, "Hey, Night Walker is that you?" He says, "Hey, sister come on and sit down beside me."

Sister and Dolly knew more about the streets than anyone could even get close to, and with Dolly gone, he had to rely on sister. She has been on the streets for thirty years and was a schoolteacher at one time.

Somehow, she gets a little check each month, and it goes to a lawyer, and he cashes it and gives her the money.

As they are visiting, he asks her, "Has anyone ever tried to rob her?" She tells him that about two years ago, the guy who was always hanging around Dolly followed me one night, and he stops her and says, "The guy who was stabbed to death by the ferry landing?"

She says, "Yep, and here is what I used." She took out a knife that had about a six-inch blade, and it was razor sharp. He says, "You go, girl." They talk until nearly daybreak, and he heads to his apartment and sends Nancy a text asking her if she thought she could get some time off.

As he wakes up around two, he sees a message from Nancy saying, "Call me when you wake up." He gives her a call, and she has talked with the acting chief, and he told her that it would be ok with him for her to take some time off if she would keep her phone on so he could always get in touch with her and yes, "I am ready to go."

He calls Lester and they plan to meet later and talk about the trip. With it being in the let's think about doing this to loading up, some things need to be done.

The next morning, he takes Lester to meet the acting chief and gives him a quick recap of his military background, being homeless and owning a pie and sandwich shop in Key West. After all of that, he has a police officer ID from the city of New Orleans just to be on the safe side if they get stopped.

Now that both bikes have rather large saddle bags, the girls can have one and the guys the other, and they plan on stopping every third night at a motel that has laundry for their customers to use or one of the major truck stops.

Two days later, they are on the road. They go down the west coast of Florida thru Tampa, St. Pete, down to Marco Island, across Alligator Alley and then down to Key West. Their first stop was to see the people who had bought their pie and sandwich shop. It was a great reunion.

After three days of sun and surfing, they headed up the west coast of Florida. Miami, Palm Beach, Jacksonville, and into South Georgia headed to Savanah.

Just as they cross into Georgia, they get stopped by a local officer. As they are getting out their license, the officer says, "Where do you boys think you are going?" Just then Lester says, "BOYS?" Lloyd says in a flash, "Settle down, Lester it's ok."

They let the officer check out their license and want to go through all of their clothes, and that is when they both show him their New Orleans police IDs and Lloyd says, "Excuse me, does this help?"

After they do that, he wants to be their best friend. An hour later, they are back on the road. Lester is still mad. Savanah, Atlanta, Birmingham, McComb and then home. Once there, they all scatter in different directions.

He picks up a few groceries from the corner store in the Quarter, and he stays in his house for two days. Friday night comes around, and he is out on the streets.

Football games in the dome will mean a lot of people in the Quarter and a lot of stuff happening. Drunks, fights, pickpockets and ladies of the night. He loves it. When he sees a known pickpocket person, he will ease up to them from the back and stick his I D in their face, and he suggests that they get out of the area. It works most of the time, and then when the ladies start talking to him.

He acts like he does not know that they are working ladies and lets them make him all kinds of deals. Once they think they have got one, he produces his ID, and after that develops into some saying, "Oops, see you later," and then there are the ones that do not appreciate him taking up their valuable time, and he gets a very nice cussing.

Life is good. He and Lester take a lot of day trips, and sometimes they are gone for a couple of days. The General has told Lester that he will be going into assisted living and that he will be selling his home, but whoever buys it has to let him stay there as long as he wants to or needs to.

Daniel calls and tells him that they have enough evidence to make a raid on the house in McComb, and they know there are some people from New Orleans involved, but they don't know just what their part is. They may be helping with distribution or breaking big lots down into smaller lots or what, but we will be hitting them and hitting them hard and quick.

Then he gets a call from Tucker, and he is telling him that they have had two undercover people working in Mobile and Baton Rouge and one in New Orleans, and the agent in New Orleans goes by the name of Junior. He nearly drops his phone and decides to get in touch with his friend, the chief and just tell him to stop what he is doing and take the cash and run and also that he needs to retire and move somewhere else like Prescott, Arizona.

He goes to the chief's apartment and tells him that they need to go to dinner, and he is driving. They are in his new truck and headed to Rico's and the table in the back corner.

After they have ordered, Lloyd says, "Now listen to me, and I don't want any questions, and when I get through with you all, I want you to say, ok, I will start the process tomorrow and thanks for being my friend."

The chief has no Idea what is going on, and he is really too nervous to even think about eating whatever it was he ordered.

Lloyd leans over and says, "You will stop whatever it is you are doing in Mississippi and you will start your retirement paperwork tomorrow and as soon as it is in the system, you clean out your apartment and find some place to move to because a lot of people are going to jail for a really long time and I don't want you to be one of them do you understand?"

He finally manages to say, "Yes, I do, and where should I go? He asks him if he had ever been to Arizona, and he says no, but he has always wanted to go there and possibly retire there.

"Good answer," he says. "Here is the number of a guy who lives there and at one time lived here. He is currently living by himself, to the best of my knowledge. When you call him, tell him you are a friend of mine, that you need to get out of here, and that you will be on the road within the next couple of days."

He and Lester help him pack up his new truck and wave as he leaves the city on I-10, headed west.

Nancy has started dating the new assistant chief, and Sally has moved on to greener pastures somewhere and they have found their sister dead from what looked like natural causes.

As he and Lester are sitting in his apartment, he takes down his old Atlas and says, "Where are we going? When do we leave here?" Lester opens the Atlas to Louisiana and puts his finger on Natchitoches and says Right there."

The last anyone had heard about them was that they had a house with a big porch facing the river and singing, "Man, life is Good especially when you own a pie and sandwich shop."

After two years of bliss and his partner getting married plus the New Orleans police chief keeps calling and asking him when he was moving back to the city, he and Lester talk. They decide that he should go back to the city, and his new wife can help him in their money-making sandwich and pie shop, and then Lester says I have a deal for you that you can't turn down.

"Since we used your money and mine, you own half of the business. We have never had any questions about the boss or owner, so here is what I am going to do—and you are going to take the deal, and there will not be a discussion about it. Do you understand?"

Lloyd says, "Yes, I do."

Lester tells him that he will send him a check at the end of each month until he has gotten his initial investment back, plus another six months of half the pretax profits, and then he asks, "Do you want me to help you pack, and how are you going to get all of your stuff on you motorcycle?"

He moves back into his old apartment in the quarter. With him being gone for two years, there are a lot of night people in the quarter who have no idea who he is and who he knows.

Once he gets settled, he has lunch with the new chief of police, sheriff and district attorney. They all have stories to tell him about and try to bring him up to date on what has been going on, and they are really concerned about the current wave of homicides and influx of dangerous drugs.

He tells them that he probably can't do much about the homicides, but as far as the drug problem, he just might be able to find out who and where the base of operation starts there.

His contact at the FBI has retired but wants to meet him for lunch and introduce him to a couple of new agents who are based out of the New Orleans field office.

Daniel with the DEA, has been promoted to area supervisor and is really hard to catch up with. The new DEA director based in New Orleans has really turned things around, and even with her making headway in the drug market, it is still a problem.

As he adjusts his body clock to being awake at night and sleeping in the daytime, he feels it is time for a little night walking, so he heads out the door. His first stop is Café Du Monde, the world-famous coffee-and-beignets meeting place. It still draws people from all over the world who want to say they had coffee and beignets in the French Quarter. Oddly enough, it was the Spanish who built the now-famous French Quarter—but people don't need to know that.

He walks down to the end of Esplanade, where it ends at the docks and just hangs around watching and listening as he is starting to move toward the downtown side of the docks. He hears this voice saying, "Hey Lloyd, is that you?" He stops and waits and says, "Yes and who wants to know?"

The voice says, "Hey, it's Buddy, and I heard that you were back walking the streets. Where have you been?" Lloyd tells him that he has been trying another way of life and had decided that he needed to get back to the city and try and keep the bad guys away. Buddy says, "Well young man, you are going to have a full-time job doing that." He asks him what he meant by that, and he says that there are a lot of drug people coming and going around the docks and a lot of foreign people coming and going.

As he is starting to move on, he tells Buddy, "You don't need to go run your mouth and tell everyone that I'm back. Here's twenty bucks— so keep your mouth shut. And by the way, if you think you hear something that I should know, come and find me."

As the sun starts to rise and the fog off the river covers the Quarter and the night sounds start to fade, he feels right at home again, and he has really missed the area.

Just as he starts to head toward his apartment, gunshots ring out close by. He stops and listens, and waits to see if there is any wailing and crying. He hears nothing and decides just to stay backed up into a doorway where Decatur Street ends.

Hearing nothing for twenty minutes, he leaves the doorway and starts walking toward his apartment. The street sweepers and garbage trucks start their morning routes, and he keeps heading to his apartment.

Chapter 6
Quarter funeral

He gets up when he hears the funeral procession moving through the quarter. As soon as he can get dressed, he is in with everyone walking to the cemetery. The whole time, he is keeping an eye out for someone that the city just may be looking for or someone he knows that is up to no good.

After the graveside service, the procession heads back through the quarter playing lively music, and the umbrellas are swinging and twisting. Everyone is in a joyful mood. Then the gunshots ring out, and everyone starts running in all different directions.

He steps into a doorway and tries to get the bearings of just where the shots came from, and looks to see if there are any bodies in the street. There is nothing in sight, but who knows what is on the side streets?

Now you hear the sirens and cop cars going everywhere. By the time they arrive, the streets of the quarter are empty and hardly anyone is in sight. Once they see him, they automatically start asking questions. He was no help.

Once they don't find any bodies lying in the street, they find somewhere else to go, and he always wonders where they are in such a big hurry.

Having not eaten anything since late yesterday, he decides to go and have a few raw oysters and then some spaghetti later tonight. As usual, his favorite oyster bar is always crowded, and if he can't get to the bar, he has his special table in the far back corner, and even after being gone for a couple of years, the wait staff is still the same and they know what he wants.

As he is taking his time eating, a guy sits down at his table and says, "Hi, I am a friend of Brown's your old FBI buddy and when he had heard that you were back in town, he told me to look you up and visit and so here I am, and I am visiting, and I hope you don't mind." He tells him that any friend of Brown can sit at my table anytime, and just how is Brown doing in retirement, like he never did too much when he was working?

Brown's friend introduces himself as Jim Hebert, and he has been an agent for fifteen years and was born and raised in Lafayette and has been working in the area for just over a year. They talk for a few minutes and Jim leaves, and they are going to meet at Lee Circle tomorrow at three.

Once through eating, he decides to go and get some coffee and check out Jackson Square. There is always someone walking around the area. Tourists as well as locals, and then here come the bums and homeless people. It has always been a meeting area for the good as well as the bad. He has learned a lot of things while sitting in the area.

Then he decides to go and see Mr. Romero; the old Italian candy maker since he has not seen him since he got back in town. When he walks in, Mr. Romero comes from behind the counter and gives him a really big hug and asks him did he wants a free piece of candy or a fresh pastry? He refuses, and they talk for a bit.

Mr. Romero tells him, "Some of the people coming into town on the airplanes that come into my shop have been seen with some known drug people. They buy lots of pastries to take back to other towns with them, and I've seen them exchanging packages right at my front door. They always pay with a handful of big bills, and I really like their business. They're here every Thursday right after dinner. Even last week, the airline people were riding in a big, fancy black car instead of a cab, and they stayed parked right in front while doing their business."

He tells Mr. Romero, "I want to work behind your counter this week to learn a little about the business, and then I will take care of the airline people next week and you can take a little rest." Mr. Romero tells him, "I have worked every day for the last thirty-one years, and the only time I took off was when my wife died and when the hurricane flooded everything." Then he says, "Can you come back after I close and listen to what I have to say?" He tells him, "I will see you at five minutes after eight when you close."

Just as he is starting to lock his doors, Lloyd steps up and lets him in, and they go into the back of the shop where Mr. Romero lives and bakes all of his goods.

They share some really strong Italian coffee and pastry. Then Mr. Romero says, "You know my friend, I have no relatives here in the states, and I think I want to go back home to be with my people, and I have lots of money, and I own this building." Automatically Lloyd thinks, there is no telling how much the building is worth.

As they are talking, Mr. Romero gives him a copy of his bank statement, and he has six hundred thousand dollars in his checking account. Then he says, "Let me show you something." He pulls the rug back and has a wood box under the floor, and when he opens it up, it is full of cash. Now he gets nervous and thinks, Man, I'd better get him a lawyer that can be trusted, get this building sold, his funds transferred into something safe, and then try to get him back to the homeland."

He calls Jim and tells him that he cannot meet with him, and he will check with him once he has some time.

Larry Little is an attorney who had helped him in the past, and he was a one-man show and could be trusted because they had done some stuff together in the past. He gives Larry a call, and he says that he had heard that he was back in town and was wondering how long it would be before you called.

He tells Larry that he would see him at nine in the morning, and if he had anything planned to cancel it. He says, "ok."

Now that Mr. Romero has scared the hell out of him, he decides to go home and try and get some rest. Three hours later, he is out the door going to get some coffee and see what is going on at midnight.

He takes a walk on Canal Street on the trolly tracks. He does not like walking on the sidewalks because bad things can happen. After a good walk, he is in bed at three and will see Larry at nine.

When he walks into Larry's office and before Larry can even get up to shake his hand, he puts his pistol right in the middle of his desk and then Larry says, "You have not changed a bit and here, look at my new Glock 43. Just got it last week, and it really shoots good."

After all the hugging and hand shaking, Lloyd says, "I have just discovered that Mr. Romero is as rich as the Rockefellers and owns his building and is now wanting to go back home to his homeland." Larry says, "Ok, I will buy the building and now what?"

Lloyd tells him how much he has in the bank, and that there is no telling how much cash he has under a rug in his kitchen. Larry says, "You will have to get with your FBI buddies to get him a passport. I am sure he will need someone to travel with him and keep tabs on all of his financial stuff. Is your passport current?" and he tells him, "Yes, it is." Then Lloyd tells Larry about all of the transactions that are going on in and in front of the candy store.

Larry says, "Let's get him back home, and then maybe you and I can operate the candy store and possibly catch some of the big bad boys and girls if they are involved, and maybe they will need an attorney." Lloyd says, "Yes, they might need a good one."

He gets with Jim at the FBI and tells him that we need a passport for Mr. Romeo at the candy store because he wants to go back home to be with his people, as he is getting up in age. Jim says, "Give me his full name, birthplace and birth date, and we will go from there."

The next day, when the candy store opens, Lloyd tries to get all the info from Mr. Romeo that Jim needs. He finally manages to write down the city in Sicily where he was born, the estimated birth date and a few other things.

Now Lloyd has to start working behind the counter to try and learn all he can, so when the airline people come in, he can wait on them and give them what they want. Mr. Romero had told him, "They usually buy ten to twelve dozen pastries and then take them back up east and sell them to the shops there, and I think they are attaching some of the drugs inside the boxes or just adding them to whatever they are using to distribute their goods."

Somehow, he wants to get the license number off the car that they arrive in. He decides to have Mr. Romero take a walk around the corner and get it for him. He probably has not been outside the shop in a really long time. When he asks him how often he gets out, he says, "I only get out to go to the bank or corner store to buy a few groceries, and I do that every Sunday morning after going to mass."

He and Larry get with him, and he signs over a power of attorney to help take care of everything, and then he starts the process of Larry buying the building. The next thing was to get it appraised, and his friend was going to do that next week.

Now that he has spent some time behind the counter, he thinks that he knows what he is doing. Sure enough, right after lunch on Thursday, the big black car pulls up front and three flight attendants get out. When they see him behind the counter, one says, "Hey, where is the little old man that is usually here?"

He tells them, "He has gone to the bank, and Mr. Romero will be retiring and moving back to the old country. He is teaching me how to make everything, and I will be glad to take care of your needs. We have fourteen dozen of the pastries ready for you, and I will put them in the car."

As he is taking the boxes out, he sees Mr. Romero looking around the corner, getting the plate number. As he is putting the stuff in the back seat of the car, he recognizes the driver as a big-time hoodlum and part-time drug runner. He knows who his boss is and where they hang out sometimes. He did not see Lloyd.

When they leave, Mr. Romero comes in and gives him the plate number and says, "You did very well, my boy and when I leave, I am giving you the candy store for helping me go home, and I want you to go with me to meet my people and help me take care of some business in the homeland."

Now he is thinking, "I have never been out of the states, and I really don't know if I want to go but if my friend wants me to go with him, I guess I will do it."

Mr. Romero, Larry and Lloyd try to get everything done while still trying to keep the candy store operating for their regular everyday customers. Larry says that they need to start training in how to make the pastries and hard candy that Mr. Romero has been making, since who knows when.

As they are going over everything, Larry says, "With him no longer here, do we still need the candy store and with me buying the building, that will allow me to have some good renters in there." They decide to tell Mr. Romero their plans, and he tells them that if that is what they want to do, it is ok with him because he will be leaving soon, and he will be a long way away from the French Quarter.

When the news got out about the candy store closing, the city went crazy. The governor even got in on the action by saying that he went there as a kid and talked with Mr. Romero. All of the T V stations are there wanting a story. He asks Larry to talk to them.

With all of this going on, he thinks, "How am I going to get involved or finding out stuff about the drug thing that is going on and if and when I do find out something, who can I get to help me, but I will figure it out.

They make the announcement when the store will be closing, and a lot of town people stop by and buy whatever is left and give Mr. Romero a big hug.

He takes time out to check out the plates on the big black car that always brings the airline people to the store, and it is registered to a real-life bad guy who lives across the river. If he is not the king of the local underworld, he is right close to it, and with everyone knowing who he is and what he does, no one can seem to catch him or any of his people, but that just might change in due time.

They go to the bank and do all of the necessary paperwork to get his funds transferred into a bank in Sicily. Mr. Romero is on the phone with the bank president telling him that he is coming home and that he had better take good care of his money. Having Larry do all the legal stuff sure was a help, and he got the building at a real bargain because Mr. Romero said that he did not need the extra money.

The store is closed, and Mr. Romero's belongings have already been shipped, and he and Lloyd are headed to the airport to fly to New York, Rome and then to a small airport on the island of Sicily. After eighteen hours, they finally reach their destination. At least they flew first class, and that made the trip easier.

Half the island must have heard that Mr. Romero was coming home, and there were probably a hundred people waiting for him to get off the plane.

After ten days of touring the island and meeting all of his relatives, he is ready to come home. He knows it is going to be a tough time leaving Mr. Romero, but life goes on.

Once home, he decides to just stay in his apartment for a couple of days to adjust for the jet lag and try and figure out how he can find out something about the drug thing now that the candy store is closed, and the flight people will have to make other plans, and he wants to know what those plans are.

Before he gets too interested in the drug business, he decides to take a trip and go see Lester and his wife and see how the sandwich and pie is doing. He gets his bike serviced and heads out. Not having ridden in a while, he stops every hour or so and walks around because his back injury has not gone away.

He has a good visit, and Lester and his new wife are really doing well. They have become very involved in the community and are on the board of the Christmas committee. As he is getting ready to leave and head back home, he gets a call from Daniel, his DEA buddy he had met in Biloxi, the one he had helped get his friend the police chief to go straight and stop hanging with the wrong people.

Daniel tells him that the current DEA agent in charge of the lady from Houmas has decided to retire, and he has been promoted to her position. He will be moving into the city within the next thirty days, and he looks forward to running the streets with him.

Back home, he goes through all of his mail, and he has three offers for free hearing aids and a special program on cremation. All junk mail goes directly into the trash.

He usually gets his insurance settlement check, which is a direct deposit into his account, about this time of the month, so he checks his statement out. When he sees his balance, he thinks, man there has been a mistake, and he'd better call the bank. He sees that it was a cash deposit at about the time he and Mr. Romero were doing all of his banking stuff, and he calls the girl who was helping them.

When he gets her on the phone, she says, "I thought you might be calling because Mr. Romero somehow got his hands on one of your deposit slips and made the deposit the day you were here helping him." Then she said that he had made one for Larry, but not anywhere close to what you got, and he really was a nice man, and the city will miss him.

He calls Larry and they have a long conversation about him and what a nice guy he was, and Larry says, "Why don't we go and visit him next summer?" Lloyd says, "Man that is a really a lot of flying and Larry says, "Let's use the money he gave us to fly first class," and Lloyd says, "I will have to think about that and goodbye."

The drug thing is on his mind a lot. He sure would like to put the screws to the bad boy across the river, and now that Daniel is moving to town, together they just might be able to do something.

Jim, the FBI agent, calls and tells him that he had just heard that there was a new DEA agent in charge moving into town, and he is hearing that all of the other agents are glad because the gal that was here was really not a nice person, and she stayed gone most of the time, and they liked that.

Lloyd does not tell him that he knows Daniel, and he thanks him for the information. He sends Daniel a text saying the word is out on the streets, and the bureau is glad to have you coming to town.

Before he can do anything else, Jim calls him back and asks him if he could have dinner with him and the agent in charge because there is something he wants to talk to you about and if you do it, it just might help me down the road.

They meet at the Pasta House on Broad Street, and as usual, they seat him in the back away from everyone. While they know him, they have no idea what he does, but they do know that he is a night person, and the owner always tries to comp his meals, but he always pays.

The agent in charge's name is Tucker, and he is from Kansas City and was transferred into New Orleans from the Denver area. And has been an agent for twenty years, and before that he was a Navy SEAL. Seems to be an alright guy, but time will tell.

As they are having dinner, Tucker asks him did he knew anything about a group of bad guys across the river that at one time was meeting, and there was a shootout, and an informer for the bureau was hurt? Lloyd says, "Yes, that was in the Gretna area, and I think a couple of the guys bought the farm, and why are you asking?"

Tucker tells him that the group has started up and asks if he knows anything about them, and if he would be interested in trying to meet some of the people and if so, we will be glad to take care of you with a nice sum of cash.

Lloyd says that he knew the informant who got shot there, and he has moved away, and he was not interested in messing with them. "But I do know someone that just might be your guy, and I will start looking for him. If and when I find him, I will let you know."

When he is walking back to his apartment, he is thinking, Man, working at the sandwich and pie shop sure was nice, and even spending time with Mr. Romero was better than all of this. I wish I could just stop trying to be Dick Tracey and settle down somewhere.

Just as he gets to his apartment, his phone rings, and he sees that it is Nancy. When he answers, he says, "Yes, I am a tired and lonely man, and I don't have any friends. Oh please, pity me." She says, "You should be lonely, and how about lunch tomorrow—or better yet, dinner, and I am buying."

He says, "See you at Duke's at six."

He stays in all day taking naps and checking the news on his phone and decides to turn his computer on and see if the president of the country has tried to get in touch with him.

As he is checking his email, he sees one from Mr. Romero. He tells him that his grandson got him a computer to play with and writes, "I really want to thank you for helping me close up shop and get back to the homeland. I am loving it, and I have found a girlfriend. Please try and come visit me soon."

He answers him back, saying that he enjoyed his email and that he is thinking about retiring and just might move over there and live with him. Mr. Romero answers back, saying, "My new house overlooks the ocean, and I have plenty of room."

When he sees Nancy, his heart has a little flutters. He had always cared for her but just did not want to settle down. But now that he is older, he just might consider it—but here in New Orleans. Every time he visited Arizona, he always said that it might be a good place to live.

At dinner he finds out that her marriage only lasted for eight months. He did not ask any questions but was glad to hear the news. At the end of a three-hour dinner and closing the place down, it comes to where they want to move to and when.

Having worked for the city over twenty-five years, she could retire at any time with a fairly decent retirement income. Plus, with what she had saved and invested over the years, she was in real good shape. Between the both of them—and his insurance settlement income and Mr. Romero's gift—they would not have any money worries.

She retires and they sit down in his apartment and start looking at places on his old, worn-out Atlas. After visiting six different places over two months, their top choice was Jackson Hole, Wyoming, and their second choice was Sedona, Arizona.

Once they checked out the personal tax rates in both states, he kept saying that he really did not want to pay state income and personal property taxes like he had to in Louisiana. When he was just killing time, he decided to check some tax rates in some states, and he found out that in Kansas that your personal property tax was due on December the twentieth. Right before Christmas and that had to really hit people hard.

As they are having lunch, he asks her did she have a passport, and she says that she does, and it was current. He tells her that he was just thinking about something, and he will tell her later. She tells him that she did not have any idea what he was thinking, but if they went somewhere foreign, she wanted it to have nice weather and be safe.

Later in the day, he starts looking into more about Sicily. While there with Mr. Romero, he really enjoyed the climate, the beaches and most of all the people. He was amazed at the number of people there spoke English, and he felt safe just walking the streets in daytime as well as at night.

He gets in touch with Mr. Romero and asks him to try and find a place that they could rent for a few months. Five minutes later, he gets a reply from him telling him that the house next to him that overlooked the ocean was for rent, and when was he coming to see him?

Now he sits and thinks, here I am walking the streets at night and doing nothing. The FBI wants me to get involved in something, and Daniel is not here in charge of the DEA. He was sure that he would be asking him to help. Sadly to say the crime in the city had just about gotten out of hand like other big cities, and his only close Friend was Lester, and he was nearly two hundred miles away, why not take a trip and see Mr. Romero.

Once in Sicily, as they were walking along the beach just as the sun was setting, she stopped him and said, "I sure hope you are planning on staying here with me because I am not leaving for any reason."

Life is good on the island.

Moving back.

Once they are settled into their apartment overlooking the beach and ocean, things are great. Every Monday and Thursday, they take language lessons trying to learn how to converse with everyone. Wednesday is spent walking around the countryside, and they try and go fishing on Fridays and Saturdays is a trip to the open market and church on Sunday.

A lot of times, after language lessons, they go to the beach and walk around and might get ankle deep in the water. This day, he threw some water on her, and the game was on. He waded out into the deeper water, and she would not follow him. He kept teasing her and asking her to at least get her knees wet.

After a few minutes, she had managed to get her knees wet, and he went and gave her a big hug from the back, and she flinched and said, "Wow, that really hurt my breast, and I guess it is nothing. That did not sit well with him, and when they were back in their apartment, he told her to do a breast massage and check if there possibly could be a lump or something else in it."

After a self-exam, she discovered what she thought was a lump, and the area was very tender. When she tells him about the area, it was settled that on Monday they would try and see a local doctor and if not they would try and see one on the mainland.

The local doctor suggested that they go to the mainland, and he would make them an appointment at the hospital, and they would put her in touch with the right doctors. They were to be there on Tuesday at eleven. They went over the day before and had dinner, and checked out the town.

After the doctor's visit, he suggested that they go back to the states and be seen by doctors in New Orleans at the Ochsner Cancer Center.

They both felt weak in the knees and started making plans. Three days later, they were in New Orleans at the famous cancer clinic.

After two days of X-rays, MRI's and exams, her doctor said that she should be scheduled for surgery as soon as possible, and he would get that done. He called them later in the day, and her surgery was scheduled for Friday at one o'clock. All they could do was just look at one another.

He finds Lester and gives him the news, and he will be at the hospital when they get there. They took a walk in the quarter and then tried to get something to eat, but neither of them was hungry. They went back to his old apartment and tried to get some sleep, but they could not, and they just laid there and talked.

They arrive at the hospital at eight, and Lester is waiting. They prep her and take her back to surgery at noon. As they are taking her away, the last thing she says is, "Okay, now you two boys do not get into any trouble, because everyone that we knew at one time is not here, and I love the both of you."

Two hours later, the doctor comes out, and when he sees both of them, he tells them to come with him into a side room. Once inside, he tells them to sit down and pay close attention to what he has to say. Lloyd breaks into a heavy sweat, and Lester says, "Hold on just a minute, doctor." Then he tells Lloyd, "Just because the doctor started by saying that, it does not mean doom and gloom."

The doctor starts by saying, "I am sorry, but doom and gloom just might be a way of delivering some not-so-good news. Once we opened up your wife, we noticed that the cancer in her breast had covered most of her chest cavity, and the only thing we could do was close her up and try to make her comfortable."

Lloyd throws up, and Lester grabs him. The doctor says that he will go and get him some water, and then he wants him in the ER for a while, and then his wife should be out of recovery.

Once in the ER, he is given an IV with some meds in it. Lester is right beside him. The nurse tells them that Nancy is out of recovery and in a room. She takes them to her room, and on the way Lester tells him, "Suck it up and look positive if you think you can." And he says, "I got it, big boy."

When he sees Nancy with all the tubes and other things around her, he gets weak in the knees and finally manages to say, Hey baby, I hope you are ready to go home because Lester is about to run me crazy." They all managed a little laugh.

The nurses ran them out of her room mid afternoon and told them that visiting hours for them was at eight in the room because she needed some rest now get out of her. He kisses her, and they are gone.

Once in Lester's nice new car, Lloyd goes limp and starts shaking and crying. He just lets him cry himself out. Once he gets control of himself, he looks at Lester and says, "Why did this have to happen to her and not me?" And Lester says, "Hey, bubba, I heard the very same thing when I was in that damn war, and no one could ever give me the right answer. I am sorry, but I can't answer your question."

They managed to eat a little, and Lester spent the night with him, and they planned to be at the hospital at eight. Neither of them got much sleep.

As they were headed to her room, they saw her doctor and he said, "I am very sorry to share this with you. Still, your wife has taken a turn for the worse, and I really don't think she will a couple more hours and I a truly sorry to have to give you this kind of news. She will wake up for a couple of minutes and then drift off, and the Hospice nurse will keep you informed.'

When he looks at Lester he says, "Please don't ask me why, because like I said earlier, no one can answer that question, and I am guessing someday we will know the right one."

Once in the room, neither one knew what to do or stand. The nurse told them to hold her hand, and when she wakes up, she will see two really nice guys standing by her bed.

When she woke up again and opened her eyes, she rolled them around and managed to smile with all the tubes in her nose and mouth. She managed a smile and whispered, "I love you, and closed her eyes and died. Lester knew but did not realize it until he came around the bed and said, "Bubba kiss her and let's go home."

They walk down to the river and just sit and talk about everything. Finally, he says, "I don't know anything about funerals and people dying, but she had told him that if anything ever happened to her, she wanted to be cremated and he ashes scattered along the beach in front of our apartment in the old country.

Lester tells him, "I will take care of that. You will carry her ashes in the parade, and when we get to the cemetery you hand them off to me and I will place them in the crypt. Once everyone has started back to town, I will take them to your apartment and just wait for you."

Once the parade started and the music was going, the dancing and umbrella waving started, and he noticed how big the attendance was. With her being a former city employee, everyone knew and loved her, and that was the reason for the big crowd.

As he was trying to get started over and get his bike shipped, he decided to fly back and try to get started in the right direction. He packed her ashes in his carry bag and managed to get them through security and headed to what he is now calling home.

Once home, he waits a few days for the local priest to have enough time to have a simple service on the beach. The day that they spread her ashes, the wind was blowing outward, and her ashes were gone never to be seen again, but he felt like she was there with them.

Two weeks later his bike arrived, and he started his plans to see as much of Europe as he could. With all his saddle bags packed, an extra one on the back seat and his backpack, he was guessing that he was ready. He went to the boat landing to wait to be taken over to the mainland and start in a northward direction.

Three weeks later, Lester met him in Paris and had rented a bike and they were on the road again together.

Author Info

Gene Gallien was born and raised in a very small town in East Texas and moved to New Orleans in the early sixties. Culture shock is not the word for his change of lifestyle.

He came to know and associate with a lot of the type of people that he wrote about. Some fiction and some nonfiction.

After 45 years in the corporate world and 17 moves, he retired back to the area where he was born and raised.

www.ingramcontent.com/pod-product-compliance
Lightning Source LLC
Chambersburg PA
CBHW070502170726
48291CB00008B/2618